PRIZE

LEGACY WARRIORS BOOK ONE

SUSI HAWKE

Cover Art Designed by Ana J Phoenix

Proof-editing done by Courtney Bassett of LesCourt Author Services

https://www.lescourtauthorservices.com/

Artist Wanted... Canvas ready for your Shibari expertise

Join my mailing list and get your FREE copy of Artist Wanted
https://dl.bookfunnel.com/smahgme01v

Twitter:
https://twitter.com/SusiHawkeAuthor

Facebook:
https://www.facebook.com/SusiHawkeAuthor

AUDIO LOVERS REJOICE!

Love The Lone Star Brothers? Fall in love all over again with Found in Beaumont on Audible!

* * *

Check out Susi's latest Audible releases

Northern Lodge Pack Series

Northern Pines Den Series

Blood Legacy Chronicles

The Hollydale Omegas

Three Hearts Collection (with Harper B. Cole)

Waking The Dragons (with Piper Scott)

Team A.L.P.H.A. (with Crista Crown)

MacIntosh Meadows

Lone Star Brothers

Rent-A-Dom (with Piper Scott)

NOTE FROM SUSI

Over twenty years have passed since the Legacy shifters finished the goddess Artio's quests and fixed the crack in the portal which separates our realm from that of the Fae. Artio and her sometime lover, the Seelie Fae prince Easton, have a plan to make use of this portal.

If you're new to this world, The Blood Legacy Chronicles featured a pack of mixed shifters from across the globe who were brought together with one goal—to save the world from the darker, Unseelie Fae, and even the charming beguilements of the Seelie. Too much magic isn't a good thing when humans are involved. The only thing they had in common was that each of them was a descendant from one of the thirteen original shamans who'd closed the portal back in the days when gods, Fae, and humans all roamed the earth.

As a thank you for their part in creating and sealing the portal that locked the Fae in their own realm, the goddess had gifted these ancient shamans with psychic gifts and mates who could bear children, regardless of gender. This was the genesis of the alphas and omegas, but the shifter world had long forgotten this history and the legacy descendants themselves were merely considered to be no more than myth. Until they weren't.

Skip ahead to our current time, and the goddess has a new set of quests in mind for the new generation of legacy shifters. Blessed with psychic gifts, strong friendships, and a pack that would literally go to the ends of the earth for each other, these shifters will stop at nothing to answer the call of their goddess.

Nothing in life comes easily, especially if you're doing a job for a minor deity... even if you have a fated mate at your side.

Keep in mind that the books in this series are meant to be short reads. All books will be short novellas that are meant to be enjoyed in one sitting after a long day when you need a fun escape.

It's time to settle in. Kick off your shoes, pour yourself a nice cup of tea or glass of wine, and curl up on the couch while you get lost in the story. Oh, and chocolate! You should definitely have a bit of sweets while you read too, because... why not?

xoxo, Susi

CAST OF CHARACTERS

Connor—Jaguar alpha, one of the "trips"—a powerful set of triplets who carry more psychic gifts than have likely been measured. Purple eye glow when shifted with a golden ring around the iris. Connor is a strong, confident, easygoing, and genuinely nice guy. His dads are Clark and Kent, the "super duo" from Alpha's Dream. His triplet brothers are Jonathan and Samuel.

Jon—Jaguar omega, one of the "trips"—a powerful set of triplets who carry more psychic gifts than have likely been measured. Purple eye glow when shifted with a golden ring around the iris. Jon is the baby trip. He's a wild child, funny, outgoing, and always ready to tease.

Sam—Jaguar omega, one of the "trips"—a powerful set of triplets who carry more psychic gifts than have likely been measured. Purple eye glow when shifted with a golden ring around the iris. He's the middle triplet who tends to second-guess himself. He's a bit neurotic and proud to be a geek, just don't get him started on Marvel comics. Nope, it's gotta be DC Universe, all the way.

Oni—Lion omega, bronze eye glow, clairvoyant. Oni is sassy, funny, and cute as can be... just don't try and tell him that. His dads are Jun and Tau from Alpha's Dom. He has one younger sister, Lei.

Jude—Coyote alpha, turquoise eye glow. Intuitive mentalist who sees patterns in everything like his alpha father Cody. He's a laid-back, peaceful, patient guy who's never in a hurry. Twin to Kyle, son of Cody, Ansh, and Kontar from Alpha's Charm.

Kyle—Leopard alpha, silver eye glow. Twin to Jude, he is a precognitive dreamer who sees visions. Kyle is hyper and loud, the yin to Jude's yang.

Toby—Bear alpha, purple eye glow. Toby is the youngest child of the "Spidermen," Peter and Parker from Omega's Destiny. He is intuitive yet totally goofy, accident prone, awkward, and suffers from foot-in-mouth disease. Toby is the baby brother of Faith and Destiny, cousin to "the trips."

Destiny—Bear omega, golden eye glow. Her gift is remote viewing. She is outgoing and keeps track of everyone, never forgetting a birthday. Twin to Faith, sister to Toby, daughter of the "Spidermen," Peter and Parker.

Faith—Jaguar omega, golden eye glow. She sees patterns

like her great-grandpa Frankie (Omega MC of Alpha's Wolf from the Northern Pines Den Series). She's an IT geek who can hack anything. Twin to Destiny, older sister of Toby. Mated to Phoenix, another pack "kid".

Ian—Fox alpha, green eye glow. Ian is gifted in prophecy. He's a quiet type who is happiest burying himself in a book. Son of Sean and Heath from Omega Found, younger brother of Lulu.

Lulu—Hawk omega, red eye glow, aura reader for both people and places. She is bold, artsy, and always the life of the party. Daughter of Sean and Heath, Lulu is mated to Lei and Aurora.

Aurora—Dingo alpha, royal-blue eye glow. She's gifted in telepathy or, as she calls it, "mind-speaking." Despite being an alpha, she is shy and sweet, a total introvert. Her dads are Ethan and Dimi from Omega's Mark.

Lei—Red Panda alpha, amber eye glow. Gifted in retrocognition, which means she sees past events just by touching an object or standing in a place. Lei is a techy gadget wiz, cocky because she knows her stuff, yet patient with those she loves. She's snarky and fiercely protective of her big brother Oni... when she's not directly competing with him.

Phoenix—Wolf alpha, orange eye glow. He's an object reader who is gifted with psychometry and can tell the history of an object and the emotions of people who've handled it just by touch. Legacy gifts aside, Phoenix prides himself on just being an average dude and all-around nice guy. His younger brother is Aaron, and their dads are Mark and River from Alpha's Seal. He's mated to Faith.

Aaron—Wolf omega, yellow eye glow. His gifts aren't as strong, but he's an empath who has a knack for cartography. Like his dad, River, Aaron is a total hippie who's all about peace and balance. His wolf isn't happy with his vegan proclivities, but he's working on that.

CHAPTER 1

CONNOR

"The only good thing about the dads making us go to a human university is getting to celebrate finally being done." Jon held up his beer with a triumphant grin. "'And on that note, I toast to our freedom."

"Whatever," Lulu giggled as she held her fists to her eyes and mimed crying. "Like you guys ever let school tie you down anyway. Poor baby Jonnie... he had to go away to university and get a quality education."

"Be nice, sweetheart. You wouldn't have liked it if we'd been separated for a few years. It couldn't have been easy for the trips to be away from all of us while they got their degrees," Aurora chided her mate.

"Please." Their other mate Lei shook her head. "I think they spent more time coming home to visit than they did in the dorms. Oh wait, the super-rich, super-powerful psychic trips didn't have to live in a dorm. Their grand-daddy bought them a nice condo to live in, remember?"

My brother, Sam, shook his head. "It wasn't like that, and you know it, Lei. Our granddads wanted to make sure that we had privacy to shift and use our powers if we needed to, and that wouldn't have been possible in a dorm situation."

"Don't defend yourself to these wenches, Sammy. Especially to Lei; she's just jealous." I ducked with a laugh when Lulu threw an apple core at my head in defense of her mate. Even while I teased, I kept one eye on Oni—the omega who owned my heart, even if he didn't know it yet.

It was nice to be sitting here on the beach with a bonfire crackling and the company of my brothers and our friends —our pack, really. Our families had been close for so long, our respective parents felt we were more like a pack than anything else, despite the varied mix of shifters repre-sented among us.

"We should tell ghost stories or something," my cousin Faith said from where she was curled up on her mate's lap. Phoenix nodded his agreement as he snuggled her closer.

Jude shook his head. "I don't think any of us are capable of being frightened, so why bother? Between all of our psychic gifts, we've all seen some shit—especially the triplets. Hell, they've probably already seen this conversa-tion play out."

"No, although we probably could have if we'd wanted to

peek into tonight's forecast, as my brothers and I would call it. But we can't see exact conversations and outcomes, only probabilities. Free will, you know? The future is always in flux." I shrugged as I tried to explain what we'd already tried to describe to our friends a million times over the years.

Oni got up and started sniffing the air as he wandered around the circle. "I don't care what we talk about or don't talk about, I just need to figure out where that fantastic smell is coming from. Did somebody throw some eucalyptus on the fire?" He stopped and tipped his head to the side. "No, scratch that—it's not eucalyptus, although it does have that same minty essence with a touch of honey. All I know is it smells incredible and my lion wants to roll around in it and wallow."

I nearly swallowed my tongue when I realized what was happening. Jon and Sammy caught my eye, both of them wearing matching Cheshire cat grins. Jon got up on his knees and made a big show of sniffing the air. "I don't know, Oni. I think what you're smelling is..." Jon took a deep breath and smacked his lips together as if tasting the air. "Yeah, that's definitely the scent of sweaty alpha and smegma, if you ask me."

The rest of our group wasn't in on the joke, so they were looking around with various degrees of confusion until they slowly started to clue in. Lulu barked out a laugh. "Smegma? Are you kidding me with that? You are such a nasty boy, Jonathan."

"I'm lost; what are you guys talking about?" Aurora frowned at her mate.

Lulu shook her head and wrinkled her nose as she explained. "Smegma is basically a fancy word for dick cheese. It's like this chalky, creamy, gunky stuff that gets stuck under their foreskins if they don't clean prop—"

Aurora clapped a hand over Lulu's mouth. "I've got the idea. No need to make it more colorful than needed." She turned to look at Jon. "Why would Oni be smelling that? From the way Lulu's talking, it certainly wouldn't smell like mint or honey."

Jonathan was laughing so hard he could barely get words out. "First of all, Lulu would have no idea what it smells like since she has never had any interest in cocks, clean or otherwise, but more importantly—"

"But more importantly," Lei interrupted, "is that it's for my brother to find out for himself. Everybody be quiet, Oni will figure it out any minute now."

Oni stopped mid-step, about three meters away from me. "Figure what out? Wait..." He looked around the group as his eyes widened with understanding. "Oh, crap. One of you people are my mate? I guess the goddess has decided that we're going to be just as inbred as our parents' generation was, huh?"

Before anybody could respond, Oni turned to look at me with a relieved grin. The two of had been flirting since forever, but only I had known of our fated match. It had been hell waiting for him to find out. Oni broke into a run, closing the distance between us quickly as he tackled me down onto the sand. Straddling my hips, he held my shoulders to the ground as he leaned directly over my chest so we were face to face. "How long?"

"Excuse me?" I grinned into his wondering eyes, reaching up with a shaky hand to brush a bit of sand from his cheek. "How long what?"

I grunted when he wiggled to get comfortable and my cock took interest in the proceedings. The last thing I needed was to catch wood in front of this group—I'd never hear the end of it. Oni was practically staring into my soul with those fathomless, nearly black eyes of his.

"How long have you known?" he demanded. "All the years we've flirted but never gone past that point, and you knew, didn't you? Tell me, Connor."

"Promise you won't be mad?" When he nodded, I took a deep breath. "For about as long as I can remember."

"Why didn't you ever tell me?" Oni sat up and crossed his arms over his chest. "Did you scent me when we were kids or is this from your legacy gift? Never mind, don't answer that. That was a stupid question. Kids don't scent their mates, of course you knew it psychically. Still, it doesn't seem fair that you knew and didn't tell me. Especially when you were my first kiss! Remember that party where we played spin the bottle and you kissed me? I hope you do, because I've never forgotten it. You were my first kiss, my first crush, my first... well, I guess you'll truly be my first everything."

"He couldn't tell you, weirdo. Don't you get it? Just like their dads, they can't share what they see or know until fate decrees it." Lei made me smile as she jumped to my defense.

"Is that really why?" Oni asked in a softer voice.

"That's exactly why," I said with a nod. "My dads taught me from a young age that I can't jump the gun when it comes to visions and future knowledge. It's not for me to tell you what the fates have planned. Do you think I wanted to wait? Fuck that! It's been hell waiting for the time to be right for you to find out. You were and are and will be my first everything too, Oni."

His eyes were sparkling as he bent over my face again, hovering mere inches away from my lips as he spoke. "So what do we do now?"

"I bet I know what he wants to do," Lulu cackled.

Oni rolled his eyes. "I think we should go somewhere more private, preferably with no commentary or interruptions."

"Good luck on that one, unless you're planning to leave the country or something. Baba is going to be *all* up in your business when he hears you've found your mate—and even more so when he hears who it is. Don't you remember how he was when Lulu, Aurora, and I got together? It's going to be worse for you, bro. Seriously, he's going to want to plan a big party and everything." Lei was laughing as she spoke.

"We could be out of Ireland in an hour; my granddads have a plane on standby that I'm welcome to use at any time." I held my breath and mentally crossed my fingers after casually suggesting that.

Oni's eyes were dancing with excitement. "Where would we go?"

I brought my hands up to his cheeks to brace his face, stroking my thumbs over his high, razor-sharp cheekbones as I spoke. "First give me a kiss, and then let's go somewhere a little more private to discuss it where there aren't any witnesses to tell our parents where we went."

His lips were touching mine before I'd even finished my last syllable. The instant spark of static electricity had him pulling back with a wince. "Is it going to be like that every time I try to kiss you?"

"Only one way to find out." I pulled his face down and tenderly brushed my lips over his before gently kissing him.

"Either get a room or get on the plane, but don't you dare hump my brother right here in front of us." Lei threw something at my leg to make us stop.

Oni reluctantly pulled away from our kiss to sit up and look over his shoulder with a glare for his sister. "Nobody invited you to watch, nosy. Go back to your sister wives and shut up." He turned and picked up the empty water bottle that was lying beside my knee. "Seriously? You threw trash at my mate? This is war, Lei."

Before he could move, I kept a firm grip on his hips. "No need to start a war, Mr. Feisty. No harm was done."

"Still," he grumbled. "It's the principle of the thing."

"Hush," Lei chuckled. "Don't get all riled up in defense of your alpha, he's more than capable of handling himself." She paused and spoke a little softer. "Shit. I'm sorry, I forgot how heightened emotions are when you first find your mate. You guys get out of here and I'll try and keep Baba up off your trail as long as I can."

Oni stood and held his hand out to help me up. I didn't need it, but there was no way I was turning it down either. I liked that my mate was treating me as an equal and not deferring to me—I couldn't have handled that from my omega. But then, hadn't I known Oni long enough to know that wasn't his style?

"This room is beautiful, but I think we've waited long enough, don't you?" Oni reached behind his head to pull his shirt off by the neck and tossed it to the ground. "We had a prime opportunity to join the mile-high club, but nooo... you wanted our mating to be special. *Wait until we get to Greece, he said. I promise I'll rock your world, he said,*" Oni singsonged as he teasingly threw my words from the plane back at me while continuing to strip. "I'm waiting, but my world hasn't been rocked yet, Connor."

"I probably shouldn't be surprised that you aren't shy in the bedroom, should I?" I chuckled as I pulled my own clothes off and kicked my pants aside. I crossed the room in three strides and lifted him easily, tossing him onto the bed with a growl as I followed him, crawling over his body to pin him down as I began kissing his neck.

"I've never been shy before, why would I start now? Is this where the world rocking commences?" He groaned as I nuzzled over his omega gland where I'd be placing my bite mark before this night was over.

"This is where our souls join and we rock each other's worlds," I scraped my teeth across his gland before licking across his chest and pushing my nose into his armpit to learn the different nuances of his scent.

My jaguar was pressing under the surface, wanting to explore, yet at the same time needing for me to move things along. I pushed my cat down, determined to enjoy every moment of this first time. As I licked my way down his abdomen to nuzzle the curly hairs at the base of his dick before licking across the crease of where thigh met hip, Oni impatiently writhed beneath me.

"I can think of other places where your mouth could go." He paused, sounding a bit unsure before continuing in an almost shy voice. "At least, I've seen it online. You do know that this is all new for me, right? I know it's weird at my age, but..."

Licking a long stripe back over the crease of his leg and up the length of his erect dick, I hovered over the tip and smiled up at him. "Did you seriously think this wasn't my first time as well?"

His eyes glowed bronze as his inner lion showed itself. "Damn. And I was about to apologize for being a virginal omega at our age. I've never heard of an alpha waiting. You weren't exaggerating about me being your first everything! I like that we get to be each other's first, last, and only."

"Not that I want to talk about my fathers right now, but they waited, and so did I. When you already know who your mate is, it would be cheating to touch another. All I could do was wait for you." I swirled my tongue around the tip of his dick and sucked it into my mouth while I stared into his eyes. To finally be able to taste, to touch, to enjoy what was mine? This was heaven.

Oni lifted up on his elbows, watching me with interest. He bit into his plump lower lip, his pupils dilated with need as a rumbling purr filled the room and the light patch of hair on his chest began to quiver from the vibration. "I love that you waited for me." His soft smile turned devilish as one side of his mouth curved into a smirk. "I bet you have a really strong right forearm though, am I right?"

I pulled away from his dick before I choked when I began laughing. "I must not be very good at this whole oral thing if you can lie there and talk shit." I sat back onto my knees, shaking my head as I absently stroked my cock. "Were you purring? I can't wait to cuddle you later and rest my head on your chest while you purr for me."

His cheeks pinked up as he began to blush. "Yeah, but don't give me shit. I'm sure you purr too. The curse of being a cat shifter, am I right? I've always said that it's not fair that our animal counterparts don't purr in the wild but we do in shifted form. It's kind of embarrassing, in my opinion."

"No, it's kinda awesome, if you ask me. I don't have to wonder if you're content or happy if you're purring, and the same goes for me. I like that some of the guesswork is taken out of things." My nostrils flared as I spoke when Oni's soft lilac scent grew stronger, its fragrance filling the air.

When I saw slick leaking between his legs, I stretched my hand down and ran it over his hole to scoop a fingerful. Oni's eyes grew wide as I brought my finger to my lips and sucked it clean. He spread his legs wider, pulling his knees up to give me a better view. "If you wanted to taste, all you had to do was ask—or take—that works too."

I growled low in my throat as I bent to answer his invitation. Pushing his legs farther back, I held his thighs in the palms of my hands as I lapped the leaking juices. Oni wasn't the only one purring at this point. My entire body was vibrating as my cat and I both reveled in the taste of our mate. I couldn't take any more, I had to have him.

Lifting my head, I paused to grind my face against his abdomen to wipe the slick glaze from my chin before I slowly prowled over his body on all fours like my jaguar wanted. I didn't stop until my thighs were flush against the backs of his legs and the head of my cock was nudging against his hole.

Oni stretched his fingers out like claws to grip my chest, sinking his fingernails into my flesh as I braced my hands on either side of his shoulders and gently began to push my way inside the heat of his body.

He sucked in a breath, his eyes fluttering closed as he winced. "Are you okay?" I paused halfway in, not wanting to continue if I was hurting him, but also not ready to stop now that we were this close to mating.

"I will be, unless you stop, that would suck." His eyes popped open as he groaned and caught my eye. "Chill. Yeah, it hurts a little—but it's like this good burn that I know is going to feel really good if you just keep going."

"That makes sense," I nodded. "I think I was supposed to loosen you a little more before getting right to it."

Oni looked like he was caught somewhere between irritation and amusement as he dug his fingernails deeper into my chest and gave a gentle, testing rock of his hips. "Less talking, more claiming. I think that would be best, don't you?"

I bit my lip to keep from laughing at my adorable mate and focused on slowly sinking the rest of the way into his welcoming heat. Once I was fully rooted inside him, I bent to kiss his soft lips while I fought to hold myself still and not move just yet. Not only did I need him to relax, but I knew if I moved even a fraction, it would be over before it began. When Oni rocked his hips again as he moaned into my mouth, I knew he was ready.

Keep it calm, Connor. Don't blow your load too soon. You've got this, bro...

I gave myself a pep talk as I slowly thrust in and out while we kissed. Oni's hands moved around to my sides and over my back, his fingernails clawing at my skin as I picked up speed.

My hips pumped a little faster, driving in deeper with every stroke. Our bodies were so close together that I felt the steel of his erection grinding against my rippled abdomen. When we both began to purr, Oni broke our kiss and began thrashing his head from side to side.

"It's too much! But not enough... I need more..." Digging his hands into the muscles of my back, Oni held me tightly against him. He panted against my ear as I nipped at his neck. "The vibrations... our purrs... holy shit... my poor dick."

It took me a second to realize what he was talking about and a laugh rumbled out of my throat before I realized it was coming. The vibrations of our purring were adding to the friction against his trapped dick. "How about if I do this." I pulled out nearly all the way then slammed back into him with a hard thrust. "Does that help?"

"More," Oni panted. "Yessss... more of that."

My cock started to tingle and I nearly came as erotic jolts shot up my spine the next time his hole rubbed against my cock as I pulled out. My cock felt like it was growing impossibly larger and I had to put more force behind the next thrust as I pushed back in.

Goosebumps broke out all over my body and my vision went white as another string of erotic tingles shot from my cock and up my spine before spreading over my body like liquid fire. "Hold on, babe. My cock feels weird," I gasped as I lifted up and pulled out.

Oni lifted onto his elbows and craned his neck to get a better look as I leaned on my arm and hip to cradle my cock in the palm of my hand as we both stared at it in wonder. His voice was reverent as my mate spoke just above a whisper. "Holy shit, is that the infamous knotting vortex that only appears between true mates?"

He sat all the way up to touch one of the nubbins that were spiraling in a row around my cock from root to just under the head. "Those look like nipples." He glanced up curiously as he rubbed the tip of his finger over one of the nubbins. "They feel like nipples too. It's weird, but cool. And in a good way, you know?"

"You're telling me." My voice cracked at the end in a high-pitched squeak. I shook my head. "Fucking hell, you try having sex while pushing a nipple-covered cock into a tight hole that's trying to squeeze the cum out of you. I honestly think I almost died for a second there."

Oni lifted an elegant brow as he gripped my shoulders to pull me along with him as he lay back down. "But what a way to go, right? Now get back in my ass and claim me with that specially textured cock. Talk about something being ribbed for my pleasure," he quipped as I carefully pushed my way back into his tight heat.

When Oni pulled my head down for a kiss, I wrapped my arms around him, holding him snugly against me as I rocked into him. This time when the electric jolts moved along my cock and up my spine, I knew what was happening and just kept going. As pain morphed to pleasure, my entire body felt like one big erogenous zone.

Hold on, Connor. Don't come yet. You can do it.

My pep talk came to an abrupt end when I realized that my cock was lodged completely inside Oni's ass. When I tried to pull out, the nubbins clung to the walls of his channel like Velcro, latching on and locking us together in my feline version of a knot. I broke our kiss and pressed my forehead against his as I gritted my teeth and tried to hold on just that much longer. But when Oni's purring increased, his entire body began vibrating to the point that the silky walls of his channel throbbed against my knotting vortex.

"Fuck... I can't..." Oni's fingernails were like sharp spikes when he dug them into my shoulder blades as his entire body tensed. His vibrating ass clenched tight around my aching cock and that was all it took. I threw my head back with a roar as I began to come. My teeth were already elongating as I jerked my head to the side and went right for his neck.

Sinking my teeth into the gland that sat in the soft spot at the juncture where neck met shoulder, I felt Oni's answering bite on my own gland as his dick shot a hot geyser of cum between our vibrating abdomens. The coppery taste of his blood covered my tongue, and the scent of lilacs perfumed my nose again while I had a trippy out-of-body experience.

For a moment there, it was as if we'd switched bodies and I didn't know where I ended and he began. I was both the vibrating ass and the fat cock with the knotting vortex that was teasing the walls of my channel. I was Oni and Oni was me as our worlds collided and we merged into one. Once I was fully encased in my own reality again, I released my teeth and licked his bite mark clean with my healing saliva.

With my mate firmly claimed, I turned to kiss him again as I rolled us over onto my back before I did something stupid like going limp and passing out on top of his smaller frame. When I heard Oni's voice clearly say *"ouch"* in my head, my eyes popped open as I jerked my lips away from his. "Did you just speak to me telepathically?"

Fuck yeah, I did. His eyes twinkled as he sent his thoughts to me instead of speaking aloud. *This is a neat parlor trick to add to your repertoire of psychic gifts. I didn't know we'd be able to speak silently. This is cool.*

I shook my head and answered him mentally. *I think this is just specific between us. But I agree, it's cool. In fact, I like it almost as much as I like your vibrobutt.*

My what? His eyes were laughing as a slow grin spread over his face.

I've heard cat omegas called vibrobutts before and I never got it until just now. Your purring is making your ass vibrate, and it's fucking awesome. I took a breath and tried not to pass out from the overwhelming sensations that already had my cock hard again.

Oh, yeah? He lifted a brow and gave his hips a slight wiggle. It was just enough to make me see stars and start coming again. Before I could say anything, Oni's lips were sealed over mine and hot cum was spilling between our abdomens once more.

"Remind me again why we're spending the day taking a tour around the ancient ruins and temples instead of staying in bed?" Oni pouted and coquettishly fluttered his eyelashes at me as we walked hand in hand up the marble steps of a large temple dedicated to the bear goddess herself, Artio. After everything our pack had experienced on her behalf at the time of our births, Oni and I had felt it was important to pay homage to her while we were in Greece.

"Because you took one whiff of yourself in the shower this morning and decided that a pregnant omega needed food and activities outside of the bedroom," I reminded him as I lifted his hand to my lips to kiss his knuckles.

Oni smiled happily as we walked into the temple. "I know, I remember. I just wanted to hear you say it out loud again. I can't believe we got pregnant on our first time out, yet our friends and family who mated before us haven't gotten pregnant yet. My sister is going to be super pissed."

"Try not to sound so happy about that, sugarplum." I gave his butt a light smack as he passed me to light a candle at the altar.

Oni looked over his shoulder with a playful glare. "Let's not have any spanking or talk of my tight *sugar plums* while we're in the goddess' temple."

I licked my lips. "I wasn't talking about your sugar plums, although I wouldn't mind sucking on those right about now. I was calling you sugarplum because you're sweet and completely mine. Plus, I need to figure out the perfect thing to call you that's just for us. 'Babe' and 'hon' are too generic."

Oni rolled his eyes with a pleased smile as he turned to take my arm and lead me away from the altar. We made our way through the crowd of bear shifters who'd made a pilgrimage to pay homage to their goddess.

I hadn't been paying particular attention to the other tourists, so I froze in surprise when a familiar-looking blond Fae stepped into my path. Then I said, "Hello, Easton. Nice to finally see you in person. Does this mean it's time?"

CHAPTER 2

ONI

I had so many questions, starting with who was that man and why was Connor asking if it was time? *Time for what?*

I realized the gorgeous creature wasn't a man the moment his skin touched mine as we shook hands and a warm, tingling sensation tickled my palm and heat spread up my arm. Now that I'd clued into that much, I quickly picked up on the fact that he had what could only be described as a supernatural golden glow about him.

It occurred to me that I had been standing there staring way too long when he shot me a playful wink and Connor got snarly. "None of that beguiling Fae shit with my mate, Easton. Let go of his hand and step aside before I bite it off." He growled low in his throat, then smiled as though nothing had happened and clapped the Fae on the shoulder after he'd released my hand. "Now come on, let's find somewhere to talk."

Easton was unconcerned by Connor's caveman alpha shit and simply shook his head. "No, not now, my friend. There are too many *others* wandering about, aye? Meet me here in the morn at that magical hour when the moon is waning and the sun begins to wake. Bring your brothers, but not their mates—it's not their time yet, or so I've been told." With that cryptic statement, he turned and walked away.

As Easton slipped away and disappeared into the crowd, I turned to Connor in confusion. "Since when are your brothers mated? And when are you going to start explaining what just happened?"

Connor took my arm and led me out of the temple. "Let's go back to our room, dearest. We can talk there."

"Dearest? Nice, but a little old-school, don't you think?" I quipped at his endearment as we made our way over a cobblestone street.

After a quick stop at the gelato cart in the lobby, Connor and I were sitting cross-legged on our bed, facing each other as he began to fill me in.

"So you've met Easton. He's a Fae prince from the Seelie court, and has been known to be a help to our pack in the past. Hmm... Let's start with dream walking. Remember how you've heard our pack talk about my dads and how they can visit other places, people, and even view past or future events in a dreamscape? My brothers and I share that gift."

"Your brothers and you share more psychic gifts than is natural, but go on." I took a bite of my peach gelato and motioned with my spoon for him to continue.

"Okay. Well, my brothers and I have had a shared vision for..." His voice trailed off as he stared down at the bed for a moment, lost in thought. Looking up a minute or so later, he shrugged. "Let's just say that we've been having the vision longer than I can remember. So basically, we've had this shared dream of being used to make the old portal that our parents sealed into a gateway between our realm and that of the Fae."

"A gateway? Why in the world would you want to do that, wasn't the whole idea of our parents sealing the portal to keep the Fae out of our world?"

Connor shook his head. "We don't know why yet, or how or even when it will happen, only that it's our destiny—what we were born to do. We've always known that it would be our mission, but even our powers are limited and we've had to wait until we were told it was time to begin. But like I said, we don't know exactly what our roles will be." He stopped and frowned. "I'm sorry, that's a lie. We have an idea of what we're going to be using it for, but I'm not free to say just yet. Even though you're my mate, this is bigger than even that when the goddess herself is involved."

"Okay, I can respect that." I paused to think as I took another bite of my cold treat. "Tell me this, though, what was that comment he made about your brothers being mated? Has something happened since we left?"

"No, they aren't mated yet. But just like me, they know who their mates are but can't say anything or act on it until the fates reveal it to their partners. Until then, they are forced to stay quiet. And don't ask, because I can't tell you either. It wouldn't be fair to any of the others, and again, it's not my right to tell before the fates decree it time."

I frowned as I remembered that moment on the beach. "It sucks that you guys know and can't say anything. I've said it before and I'll say it again, it's rude and unfair for you guys to know but not the rest of us. Am I correct in assuming that their mates are also in our circle of friends?"

Connor set his dessert aside before reaching his hands up to cup my cheeks. "I can't tell you, gumdrop. As much as I would love to, my hands are tied. Like I've said myself in the past, our powers are both a gift and a burden."

"You suck." I pouted playfully.

"Sometimes." Connor grinned as he scooted onto his stomach and craned his neck forward to slowly lower my zipper with his teeth. He looked up at me with a grin. "And sometimes I even swallow."

I spread my legs a little wider as I tilted back onto my elbows after taking one last bite of my gelato. "I think I'll need a demonstration of that, *dearest*."

As he swallowed my dick into the heat of his mouth and began to suck, I forgot all about Fae princes, portals, and plans from some goddess. The only thought in my head at this point was fuck, yeah. I loved being mated.

CHAPTER 3

CONNOR

Oni blinked a few times before the sleepiness cleared from his eyes as he stared around the empty temple. We could see between the open pillars to where the sky outside was that magical mix of silver where night met day and the stars still twinkled.

He started to reach for my hand but I put mine behind me and stepped back with a shake of my head. I realized we were as naked as we'd been in bed and quickly conjured day clothes onto our bodies before anyone joined us. Oni glanced down at his jeans and tee with a raised brow but let it go for now as he waited for me to explain.

"Okay. Well, since my brother hasn't clued you in, allow me. The first rule of dream walking is that you can't touch anyone. While this is a dream, it's also really happening on another level of existence. The construct is strong, but all it takes is for two of us to touch and it all dissipates," my brother Sam explained as he and Jonathan approached.

"What's up, big brother? Kinda rude to pull us from our beds so you could rub your honeymoon in the faces of your two unmated brothers, don't you think?" Jon smirked as he stepped a little closer, then bent from the waist to sniff Oni's stomach. "Oh, hell. You didn't waste any time, did you?"

Before either of us could respond, Easton came striding into the temple. "Hello, boys. Fancy meeting you here."

"Yeah. Fancy that." Oni smirked. "I believe you summoned my mate and his brothers yesterday afternoon for this meeting. Now that you've pulled us all out of bed, maybe you'll tell us what gives?"

Easton threw his head back with a musical laugh. He wiped his eyes as he looked at me. "Aye, he'll do, indeed. Quite the feisty little omega you've got here, mate. Did you bother to explain to the boy that he's still sleeping, and only his mind is engaged? 'Tis but a dream, is it not?" He stroked his chin and looked thoughtfully at the statue of Artio that presided over the room. "But then again, isn't life itself merely a dream? I've often thought that, myself." He stretched his arms out to the sides and spun in a circle while singing a strangely repetitive ditty in a pleasant bari-tone. "Life is but a dream... a misty, misty dream. A misty, misty dream I dreamed last night."

"Is he always like this?" Oni asked skeptically as he looked back and forth between my brothers and me.

Jon grinned. "The Fae are all like this, from what I've seen."

"Oi, and what would you know of the Fae, boy?" Easton asked with a raised brow as he dropped the act.

"More than some, less than others, I suppose. What can I say? I've seen a few things." Jon shrugged.

"Aye, I'd forgotten that for a moment. You three see many things the average mortal doesn't, do you not?" Easton rubbed his hands together. "Let's get down to the business at hand then, shall we? The magic hour has nearly passed and I'm not allowed to spend too much time loitering about."

"By whose law?" I asked curiously. "I realize you were locked in our realm when the portal was sealed, but..." I remembered suddenly that he was rumored to be Artio's bedmate. "Ah. Your lady's decree?"

Easton blushed slightly as he shrugged. "My lady keeps a bit of a leash on me, yes. But I'm free to roam, so long as I don't linger too long, use my majicks, or let myself become noticed by *others*."

"Others being humans? That makes sense," Sammy said as he nodded. "So, what made you bring us here? Is it time for us to..."? His voice trailed off as he glanced at Oni, as though uncertain of how much he was allowed to say.

Easton turned his back to us as if gazing at the coming sunrise, clasping his hands behind his back as he rocked from heel to toe. "You already know your task, but there are items needed that will work as keys. But first and foremost, you must prove yourselves worthy."

"Prove ourselves worthy?" Jon snorted. "My brothers and I are haunted by dreams and visions for a lifetime, and now we have to prove ourselves? If we weren't already good enough, why were we plagued with the knowledge beforehand?"

"Oi, surely you know how these things work, mate." Easton looked over his shoulder to flash Jon a wink before speaking in an eerie monotone as though reciting something he'd rehearsed.

> "She closed the portal long ago as
>   protection against her chosen's foe.
> But age and time the fight shall mend, so
>   the portal can open again.
> For questions you must seek answers, but
>   locks have keys you must discover.
> Two worlds at odds may join together by
>   the secrets you uncover."

"What the hell does that mean?" I asked without thinking. I noticed that Sammy had conjured his phone and was taking notes. Thank goodness for that, since I hadn't thought of it. We would definitely need to revisit this conversation later.

Easton didn't respond, instead continuing to speak in rhyme as though reciting from memory.

> "Directions four we start with east—where
>   all Earth's winds are born.
> Forbidden fruit, a warrior's golden prize,
>   lies forgotten and forlorn...
> Answer its call but guard it well for
>   without it there can be no spell."

There was a moment of silence as we all processed his words. Oni was the first to speak. "Excuse me, Easton. I beg your pardon, but you've mentioned four compass directions? And your clue would hint that we're starting with east, so that would lead me to assume that there will be three more clues or quests? But there are only three triplets. Who will be the person given the clue for the fourth cardinal point?"

Easton spun around with his jaw hanging open as he stared at Oni for a long moment. He laughed to himself, shaking his head before glancing my way. "Sure and this one is brill, mate. Be sure and keep him around."

Ignoring that, because why wouldn't I keep my mate around, I repeated Oni's question. "He makes a good point. Since this waited until I claimed my mate, and you mentioned my brothers' mates when we last spoke..." I paused to make sure I had it all. "Oh, and our parents worked in pairs too! Am I correct in assuming this will be done by couples? And if so, who the hell is the fourth couple? And more importantly, why haven't my brothers and I seen them in all the dreams and visions we've had involving the future of the portal?"

"Aye, 'tis fair to assume that an anchoring pair to your glorious magic would be needed, wouldn't you say? For now, you and your mate must begin the quest to put the steps in motion for the glorious conclusion—many lives and loves depend upon it." He stepped toward the temple stairs after that cryptic statement, as if preparing to leave.

"Wait." Sammy looked up from his phone for a moment. "Does this mean that we'll all three have our mates soon?"

Easton held his hands up and shook his head. "Easy, boyo. One step at a time, eh? Right now it's your brother that needs to shine." He headed for the steps, then paused to look back over his shoulder. "If I might make one suggestion? Be careful about biting into any shiny apples, not all of them are edible."

The four of us stood there quietly as we watched him leave. None of us moved a muscle until he'd finally disappeared into the distance. I jumped when Jonathan suddenly clapped his hands together, startling me. "Okay, now that we've had our mystical portion of the day, shall we go back to you knocking your mate up on your mating night?"

Sammy grinned at Jon's words while Oni instinctively rested a hand over his flat stomach. He tilted his head to look at me. "You guys can really smell biological changes in a dreamscape? I know that our feline noses can pick up on the slightest change within hours of insemination, but in a dream state? That's pretty cool, I have to give you that."

I shook my head. "Don't encourage my brothers, baby-cakes. It won't take much to have them boring you with more of their dreamscape exploits over the years."

"Whatever." Jon shrugged. "All I'm saying is that I can't wait to get home and tell the dads that Oni is preggo."

Oni's eyes went wide. "You wouldn't!" he gasped. "Seriously, I have four months! There's no rush. Besides, you need to let us tell everybody."

Sammy blinked at Oni for a moment before correcting him. "Five months. Feline shifters have five-month pregnancies, I thought."

Oni rolled his eyes. "Is biology really the most important thing to talk about right now? For the record though, lion shifters have a slightly shorter gestation rate. Only a month less than what you'll expect to have one day, but yeah—my pregnancy will be four months."

"That's good to know." Jon nodded. "Just when I thought we were going to get along, you go and give us a reason to be hella jelly. Although, I wouldn't change being a jaguar for a slightly shorter pregnancy. We are still the superior shifters, after all."

"As if," Oni sniffed as he and my brothers fell into the life-long argument they'd had about whose animal was cooler.

"All I know is, if you don't want Jon to blow your secret? You guys might want to cut the honeymoon short." Sammy grinned at me and Oni.

"Screw that," Oni laughed. "If you're jealous now, you should see our room. Speaking of which, I think it's time to go back there." Obviously remembering what I'd told him, he waved his fingers to say goodbye to my brothers with a playful smirk as he stretched his other hand out to grab mine.

I blinked my eyes as I found myself lying in bed back in our room. When Oni sat up and flipped on the lights, his eyes were dancing with excitement as he turned to look at me. "That was the coolest thing ever. We are *so* doing that again, right? Now tell me, were our bodies here the whole time, or did you zap us back and forth? How does that work?"

Chuckling, I reached for him and pulled him down against my chest to snuggle. "Our bodies were here while our spirits roamed free. That's why physical touch will always pull us back."

"Fascinating. I noticed not only did you apparently dress us, but your brother had a phone at one point, how did that work?" His mind was obviously working a mile a minute as he struggled to make sense of the experience.

"We can conjure anything in a dreamscape that our minds

can imagine. And yes, I will be happy to take you on many more. But first, can we maybe sleep a little longer?" I ran a hand along his back, enjoying the smooth feeling of his silky skin under my palm.

"Sure, we can sleep." Oni rolled over on top of me, crawling over my chest to sneak a kiss as he rocked his hips to slide our bare cocks together. "Or, we could maybe do something a little more interesting instead?"

CHAPTER 4

ONI

With my legs wrapped firmly around his waist, Connor shoved me against the shower wall as he pushed into me again. My vision blurred from the sensation of his knotting vortex working its way into my vibrating channel. It was too much and yet not enough... I needed... fuckkk... something more...

As if reading my mind, Connor gave one more thrust, locking his cock into my body as the heat of his cum pulsed into my channel while he sank his teeth into my overly sensitized omega gland. "Yessss... that's it," I groaned into his ear as I shot my own load between us.

After he'd caught his breath, Connor chuckled in my ear. "We didn't think this out too well. Shower sex is hot, but now we're going to be stuck here for a while."

"That's okay. Take two steps back and slowly lower yourself onto the bench, if you can do it without dropping me. We can sit there and make out while the water flows over us. Who knows, maybe we can even come another time or two."

Connor followed my suggestion and groaned as my ass continued to vibrate. "If you don't quit purring, your vibrobutt might keep us here all day."

I gave a happy sigh and continued to purr as I rested my cheek against his shoulder. Seriously, how could I not purr when I was this happy? "I love you, Connor," I sighed.

"Oni, I love you too, so much." Connor was purring now too, our chests vibrating against each other as he sought my lips for a kiss.

Two hours later, we were finally sitting down to breakfast at a charming little bistro down the docks. We'd stumbled across it while wandering the waterfront the day before, and had promised ourselves we'd stop here before we went home. After a week in Greece, neither of us were ready to leave just yet.

"Holy crap, did you try the spinach and feta omelet? It was *so* good. I like the way they served us a mini buffet of dishes. This is a great way to eat breakfast." I passed Connor a square of pastry. "I know you're looking forward to having some baklava, but you've really got to try this bougatsa. I'm a fan of phyllo dough anyway, but this mix of a sweet custard filling and the powdered sugar and cinnamon on top are going to star in my culinary wet dreams. In fact, we may have to make another trip here in the future just so I can eat my weight in this shit."

Connor groaned happily as he took a bite. "Darling, I will order the jet any time you want to come here for this. Holy cow, this is insanely good. I wonder if they sell it to-go? I would take a couple pounds of this home, if we could." We ate in silence for a few moments before he spoke again. "I'm still puzzling over what the warrior's prize could be, and how we're supposed to guard it—whatever it is."

"I don't know, but I'm sure we'll figure it out. If it's anything like what our parents went through during their tasks for the goddess, I imagine we'll have a bit of a job ahead of us that won't be solved in a day. You think we're allowed to involve our friends?" I took another bite of pastry while I waited for him to respond.

He looked thoughtful as he chewed his mouthful. "I think maybe we can. I don't know, but it feels right in my gut, if that makes sense. Maybe our generation can work together on this the way our parents did on theirs. Let's wait until we get home and can discuss it with my brothers."

I grinned. "I'd suggest another dream walk. However, not only is it broad daylight, but we have a plane to catch in a couple hours."

As I reached for the honey, the colorful three-part mural on the wall across from us caught my eye. Absently, I picked up another square of pastry and chewed it while I examined the triptych of an ancient footrace.

The first panel of the painting depicted a woman with thick, flowing hair running with a bunch of warriors in her dust, obviously trying to catch her with their outstretched hands. The second scene showed the woman being distracted as she stopped to pick up a golden apple, mindless of the fact that the warriors were getting closer. The final scene showed a warrior with her thrown over his shoulder as he held the apple up in his other hand like a trophy.

Grabbing for Connor's arm, I gave it a shake while I pointed excitedly at the artwork. "That's it! I can't believe we just happened onto this place, but I think that's our answer. These things always depict legends, right?"

Connor looked intrigued as he stood and took several pictures of the mural, then sat back down as our waitress approached. "Can I get you gentlemen anything else?" She spoke politely, flashing a bland smile, but her eyes were darting back and forth between the mural and Connor's phone as if he'd done something wrong by taking a photograph.

"Yes." Connor seemed oblivious to her reaction. "My m— er, husband and I were just admiring that artwork. Doesn't it depict a local legend?"

Her eyes narrowed as she took a step back after placing our bill on the table. "Never mind about old stories and myths. Get on with your lives, hon. Trust me, it'll be for the best if you just forget you saw this silliness."

My phone started to ring before I could pick that apart and make sense of her strange attitude. I groaned when I saw the FaceTime call coming in from my sister. Connor tipped his chin toward my phone. "Go ahead and answer it, babycakes. We've been gone a week, I'm sure the natives are getting restless."

I rolled my eyes at the *babycakes* but answered the call. "What's up, snot?"

"Are you guys still planning to come home soon?" She rushed to her point in typical Lei fashion.

"Hello to you too. And yes, we plan to come home this afternoon. Why?" I rolled my eyes at Connor. He and I both knew how intrusive my sister could be if given half a chance.

Her eyes grew larger she shook her head. "Don't do that, besides, you do *not* want to see Baba right now. Can you extend your trip? My ladies and I are on our way to join you anyway. You know we've never needed an excuse for a holiday."

"Why?" I couldn't imagine what would make her want us to delay coming home, although I wouldn't mind staying a little bit longer here in Greece.

"Dude, your flight's been rescheduled; let me just cut to the chase. Sorry, I probably should've led with that bit about your flight. But yeah, we're totally coming to meet you. How could we sit idly by and let you have all the fun after Lulu got it out of Sam that you guys are working on a cool quest? He says that you've been given a clue for some quest from the goddess. And it was delivered by a friggin' fairy prince? And he also said that he met you in a dream walk? Damn, dude. You have a lot to catch me up on. I can't believe my boring little brother is out there having such a grand adventure. First you get mated, and now this? I'm not sure if I'm jealous or just damned impressed."

Connor leaned over to see my screen. He looked like he wasn't sure which part to address first. He blinked a few times before finally speaking. "Why would Sam tell you guys that? That's not like him. And what was that about our flight being rescheduled?"

Lei blushed a little. "Hi, Connor. Umm... everyone was wondering how he knew about my brother and while Lulu was talking to him and Jon, he said that his gut told him that the three of us were meant to be there to help you. So he and Jon arranged for your plane to take us there this afternoon instead of picking you two up."

"Why was everybody wondering how he knew about me? And what exactly was it that he knew about me?" I blew off the whole flight thing, wanting to back up to the first part of her statement.

Lei laughed. "Oh, yeah. Sorry. That actually plays into why you don't want to see Baba right now. He's a little bit irritated that you not only scented your mate, but ran off and got pregnant without ever bothering to call him and Daddy with your news."

"Shit." I turned to Connor. "So much for your brothers being able to keep their mouths shut."

Lei laughed while Connor held his hands up. "Did you seriously think that would happen? Maybe if it had just been a day, but it's been a week now. That's a century in Jon time. I'm sorry, lambikins."

"No. Ixnay on that one," I muttered while my sister giggled. Lambikins indeed.

CHAPTER 5

CONNOR

Almost as soon as the girls arrived, they dove right in. They barely spared us a glance after barging into our suite and making themselves at home. Lei had her laptop out before their dust had even settled, immediately tapping away on the well-worn keyboard while Lulu and Aurora excitedly took off on a tour of the area to check out some of the local archives and museums for clues.

Oni simply shrugged and said something about not arguing with women on a mission. While he and his sister researched local legends and tried to separate myth from fact, I shook my head as I sat there and watched. I couldn't get over how smart my mate was; even though I'd known him all my life, he still amazed me with his quick wit and intuitive knowledge. I wondered how much of that had to do with his gift of clairvoyance, and how much was just down to Oni being smart as fuck.

Since there wasn't much I could do at this point, I decided a call to my dads was in order and slipped out onto the balcony for privacy. As soon as my papa's face came on the screen with my dad looking over his shoulder, a sense of well-being settled over me. The two of them had always been able to steady me, simply by existing.

"Oh, Connor. I'm happy to finally hear from you, baby. Listen, I'm so sorry I spilled the beans to Jun and Tau. I had no idea they didn't know yet." My dad spoke in a rush while Papa shook his head. For an alpha, my dad was much more sensitive than my papa.

"He wasn't thinking, son. Don't worry, he's been punished appropriately." Papa grinned. I shuddered at the secretive smile they shared. I so did not want to think about whatever that had entailed.

I carded my fingers through my hair with a groan. "Yeah, because I really needed Jun to have another reason to hate me. I don't know why, but he's always had his eye on me. It's okay though, you didn't know. Jon's the one who blabbed first anyway."

"Actually, your papa saw it in a dream, but you can blame your brother if it makes you feel better," Dad laughed. "Listen, son. Jun's bark is much worse than his bite, honey. It would have to be, right? He's an adorable red panda, how hard could he bite anyway? It wouldn't be much more than a nibble..." His voice trailed off as he grinned at the idea.

Papa laughed and picked up where Dad left off. "And yes, he's probably had his eye on you because you've always been transparent about your desire for his son. Even if you couldn't tell anybody that he was your mate, your face gave it away to anybody who was watching. How do you think your papa and I figured it out? You alphas aren't as slick as you think you are, dear."

Leaning my back against the balcony rail, I looked off into the distance at the peaceful landscape for a moment. "Do you think he'll ever accept me?"

"Connor, don't be silly. Of course he will! You just need to mend fences, that's all. Jun has never disliked you," my papa explained. "Nobody would have been good enough for his son. The fact that he's even allowed you into his home over the years shows that he trusts you. Besides, Tau adores you, so you'll have him on your side. If you ask me, he's probably just been trying to put the fear of God—or should I say, Jun—into you."

"How do I mend fences with him? The guy is like half my size but he scares the crap out of me." I cringed when I heard the whine in my voice. "Didn't he used to be a dom or some shit?"

"Yeah, but don't sweat it. It'll be easy to fix things." My dad shrugged. "He probably feels left out right now. And before this, he was probably afraid that he'd lose his son once you mated. Rushing off the way you did only cemented that concern, especially when he hasn't heard from Oni. Make a point to include him when you get home, and let him look forward to his first grandchild. Trust me, son. Once he holds that baby, he'll forget any irritations he may have regarding you."

Papa nodded. "Your dad makes an excellent point; I approve. But listen, another thing I'd like to say is that you need to stand up to Jun. He might be testing you to see if you're alpha enough for his son. I'm not saying to disrespect him. Oh dear, don't do that. But maybe quit letting him see you tremble in fear when he speaks to you. That's a good start."

I rolled my eyes as I answered sarcastically. "Gee, thanks, Papa. Now that I feel like I've been Jun's bitch all these years, I'm in a real hurry to get home."

"Hush," Papa laughed. "Besides, I'm in a bit of a hurry to meet my grandbaby too. Do you boys know if it's triplets yet? Or have you only heard twin heartbeats?"

I shook my head. "Believe it or not, it's a single birth. I realize that's not traditional in Dad's alpha line, but what can I say?"

Papa grinned while my dad looked stunned. "Your dad's parents are going to be shocked, but I say good for Oni. I was as big as a barn when I carried you and your brothers. One grandbaby is quite enough, anyway... for a start. I mean, there's always next time, right?"

Dad shook his head. "I wonder what it means that you're the first alpha in our line to not have multiples? Is this because you were a triplet and now the counter has been reset? Is it a sign of things changing in our line? There are so many questions. I need to call your grandpa Frankie and put him on this. He'll be fascinated."

"You might want to do a group call between both of your parents," I suggested with a grin. "And do a video chat, you're gonna want to see their faces when they hear that they're about to be great-grandparents."

Papa started laughing. "Oh, hell. I can't wait to see the look on your grandpapa Drew's face. He's gonna start bitching about getting old again."

I rolled my eyes at that one. None of my grandparents looked a day over forty. Thanks to the double life spans of our legacy bloodlines, we aged much slower than the rest of our shifterkin. My own fathers still looked like they were in their thirties, when they were much closer to fifty than either would probably admit. But then, when they had another century ahead of them, did age really matter?

"Connor? Did we lose you, honey? You look like you're in space over there." Papa was staring into the phone with a lifted brow.

Glancing back at my phone, I shook my head. "Sorry, I was just thinking about how young Grandpa looks. I don't know why he worries about that shit so much."

"Ooh, you're good, and likely to be cemented as his favorite grandchild after he hears that one. I think I'll wait and let you announce it to them so you can tell him just that. Besides, I suppose it *is* your news anyway," my dad said reluctantly.

"You know what? Let me talk to Oni first. Maybe we can have a big party when we get home and announce it to everybody at once. But don't say anything until I've had a chance to discuss it with my mate." I looked pointedly at my dad as I spoke.

"Don't worry, son. We won't say a word," Papa laughed.

After I got off the phone, I headed back inside to find that Lulu and Aurora had returned. The four of them were seated on the floor around the coffee table in our small sitting area while Lei showed them something on her computer.

Oni patted the floor next to him with a smile. "Join us. I think we've found the answer."

CHAPTER 6

L ulu clapped her hands excitedly, bouncing up and down as Connor took his seat. "If we have the right legend, this one involves a strong woman—and you have to know I'm on board with that one."

"But of course," Connor answered with a wry grin. "Okay, tell me the legend. I know you guys are dying to share. I feel like a jerk for letting you do all the footwork though."

I threaded my arm through his as I leaned against his shoulder. "We all play to our strengths, right? Don't worry, I think this is why we are meant to work in pairs. I had to do my part figuring out the clue, but my guess is that you'll be the one to find the object and save the day."

Lei rolled her eyes. "Because we need a male alpha to save the day? Please..."

"Play nice," Aurora chided as she leaned over to kiss my

sister's cheek. "Besides, Connor isn't some alpha caveman. He's our friend, remember?"

Lulu snorted. "Yeah, but remind me again who's the one who was able to reach the top of the Douglas fir outside of Powerscourt House in County Wicklow when we were younger? Because as I recall, it wasn't an alpha."

Connor sputtered while the girls cracked up at the memory. "That's not fair. You shifted into your hawk form and flew up the fucker before any of the rest of us had a chance."

"That's down to me being smarter, not what animal I can shift into. Your cat could've made it up there just as quick, if you'd taken the time to think about doing it in fur form. Hell, at least Jonny gave it a shot, and he's an omega like me," Lulu said with a sniff.

"Anyway..." Connor rolled his eyes. "We're getting off topic. I believe you gals were going to tell me about a legend?"

"Yes." My sister's eyes lit up as Lei glanced up from her monitor. "So the story is that there was once an awesome chick named Atalanta. She was good at all kinds of sports, especially running."

"Don't forget the part where she was a sharpshooter, a strong wrestler, and a better huntress than any of the men in her area," Lulu interrupted.

Lei held up a hand. "I was getting to that, but thank you,

dear. So yeah, she was all that and a bag of chips. But then this Oracle came along and told her that if she ever got married, she'd be screwed and lose all her skills. I guess maybe it was tied to virginity or some lame shit like that? But yeah, Atalanta's dad said she had to marry someone, because why not? Goddess forbid a strong woman should choose to remain single and not pop out a pack of babies, right?"

"You're going off topic again," I laughed. "Back to the story, if you will."

"Right." She stuck her tongue out at me and continued. "There were a bunch of men that wanted her, but nobody could have her. After a lot of pressure from her dad, she finally said that she would only marry the man who could beat her in a race, but if they lost, she'd kill them for daring to try. So naturally they all tried to race her, but she beat them, no problem. And then," my sister's eyes widened with a bloodthirsty thrill," she actually kept her word and killed every man she beat."

"She sounds absolutely lovely," Connor commented dryly. "She must have been quite the beauty for the men to line up to race her after she'd killed the first one."

"They did, though." Aurora shook her head with wonder. "Can you imagine? I've gotta say, I'm an alpha and I can't think of any woman hot enough to risk my life for." She blushed when she looked at her mates who were both staring at her with lifted brows. "Except for my mates, that is. I would totally die for them. Maybe. I mean, I would now, absolutely. But just to get their attention before we'd mated? Yeah, I'd have to think about that one."

Before my sister or Lulu could tease her, I motioned for Lei to continue. She gave her wife one last chiding look before turning back to Connor. "So there was this one warrior named Hippomenes. Atalanta actually liked him, and they fell in love. But she still didn't want to give up her powers, even for love, you know? She begged him not to race her, because she didn't want to kill him. But the idiot was determined to get her to marry him. So he prayed to Aphrodite to help him win."

"And here's where you come in," Lulu interrupted.

"I'm getting there, dear." Lei rolled her eyes at Lulu. "Okay. So yeah, Aphrodite was the goddess of love, so naturally she told him how to win. She gave him three golden apples and told him to throw them along the ground during the race. And of course he did, right? Well, Atalanta ignored the first one, but when the second one rolled past her, she paused to look at it, and that's when he had her. On the third apple, she stopped completely and picked it up to admire it, enabling Hippomenes to breeze right past her stupid ass and win the race. Can you believe that shit?"

Aurora spoke softly as she looked around at our group. "Another important note about this story is that discrimination against females was still prominent during that time, despite Greece's democracy. I think the reason this legend didn't get lost to time is because it showed that women weren't inferior and could even do better than men sometimes. And yes, she was known for being a major beauty, but then aren't all legendary females? It's not like anybody would be lining up to risk their life to marry the girl next door. But the golden apples have long been considered a myth. Most people who told the story figured it was probably just a regular apple that wasn't known in the region. Apparently, they really were actually made of gold though."

I nodded. "That makes sense, when you think about it. I mean, they were given to him by Aphro-freaking-dite. Although, I could also see where it would be considered myth because apples were used in fairy tales for evil, like Snow White's poison apple," I pointed out. Turning to Connor, I finished my thought. "And that's where it ties into the forbidden fruit from the clue. Apples were usually considered *the* forbidden fruit, right? Even back to the Garden of Eden and Eve's famous apple."

Connor nodded thoughtfully. "So are we looking for three apples, or one? Your legend mentioned three, but Easton only said something about one prize to guard."

"Exactly." I was vibrating with excitement as everything clicked together in my head. "The warrior's prize! The apple that she picked up was Hippomenes' means to win her, making both it and Atalanta his prizes. Her, because he got to marry the woman he loved, and the golden apple because it enabled him to win her. Now all we need to do is find the damn apple." I smirked at that one. "Easy peasy, right?"

Connor looked around with a wide smile as he bent his head to kiss my cheek. "So it's here in Greece then? You're right, honeybun! It will be easy. We can grab it before we go home, I bet."

I bit back a laugh as I shook my head at his cluelessness. "Connor, I was being sarcastic when I said easy peasy. Do you really think it's going to be that simple? The thing has been lost to the ages. There's no record of it even existing, which is why it's considered an object of myth. Anybody who knew about it is long dead and took the secret to the grave with them." I shook my head. "No, we need to pack up and go home. Who knows how long it will take to track this down, but my pregnancy will be over before we know it. Four months will go by faster than you realize."

Lei smiled wickedly. "Plus, you really do need to go face Baba sooner or later."

I groaned as I wrapped my arms around Connor's neck and buried my face in his bicep while my sister and her mates cackled like shrews.

Yeah... I needed to find new friends. I was pretty sure I couldn't replace my sister though, so maybe not.

CHAPTER 7

CONNOR

After we dropped the girls off at their place on our way home from the airport, we headed straight to my house. My dads had turned our property into a compound like the one my grandparents had in Belize. A few years ago, they'd built homes for me and each of my brothers so that we could all live closely if we chose. Sammy's still stood empty while he shared a home with Jon. Those two preferred to be together while I'd always enjoyed my privacy.

Oni smiled brightly when I pulled into my driveway. He leaned over and dropped a quick kiss on my cheek, then opened his door and hopped out before I could even slide out from behind the wheel. As I closed my door, I shook my head at him over the car. "You know I was planning to come around and get your door, right?"

Oni shrugged. "I appreciate the gesture, but my arms aren't broken. Speaking of which, pop the trunk so we can grab the luggage. I want to make sure our pastries didn't get smashed on the trip."

I shook my head. I should've known that my feisty mate wouldn't sit idly by while I made gentlemanly gestures. That was okay, I'd find other ways to spoil him.

After I clicked the button on my remote to open the trunk, I reached past Oni to grab the heaviest bags while he was preoccupied with checking the box with the pastries. He looked up with a relieved smile. "They're intact! Now please tell me you have freezer paper or zipper bags so I can put some of these away for later."

Leading him to the door, I set the luggage aside to unlock it. Before he could see it coming, I swept him up in my arms bridal style and carried him over the threshold. Oni kicked his feet and started laughing as he wrapped his arms around my neck. "All right, you win. Some romantic gestures have their place, I suppose. I like that you thought to do that."

I nuzzled over his claiming mark. "Of course I did. You're my omega and this is your first time coming into our home."

His hand threaded into my hair, fisting a handful to pull my face up so he could look at me. "*Our* home? Fuck me, I love the sound of that. Now kiss me, I'm pretty sure it's bad luck if you don't."

"You don't have to ask me twice," I murmured against his

soft lips before kissing him. When I finally came up for air, Oni grinned and patted me on the shoulder.

"Let me down now, caveman. I need to put these pastries in the freezer." He glanced down at his lap with a frown where the box of pastries was being smashed between us.

As I set him down, I gave his butt a swat. "Poke around in the kitchen, I'm sure you'll find whatever you need to wrap those for freezing. I'm pretty sure you will, anyway. I think I remember Sammy leaving some zipper bags here a while back. Their oven was down and he was using mine to bake. I didn't mind, because my house smelled great and I got to reap the rewards in the form of all the muffins and cookies he left for me."

While he went off to do that, I carried the luggage in and closed the door. "My bedroom is at the end of the hall on the left, I'm going to go start unpacking," I called out as I headed toward my room.

I had just emptied the last suitcase and was trying to figure out where to put Oni's clothes we'd purchased on our honeymoon when I got tackled by a flying mate. His clothes went flying from my arms as he pushed me down onto the bed to straddle my hips, smiling triumphantly as he bent to kiss me. "You know what else is traditional when a couple moves into their first home? Sex! All of the sex. We have to break in every room, it's tradition. Plus, it could be bad luck if we don't, so why risk it? I figure we can start here and work our way out to the kitchen, what do you say?"

Running my hands down his back, I grabbed his taut ass in my palms and licked my lips. "I say that I'm definitely on board with that idea." I gave my hips a thrust so he could feel my erection that was already pushing against my fly. Oni giggled as he wriggled back and forth against it.

Who knew being mated would be this much fun?

I slid my hands up under his shirt, gliding them slowly up his chest as I did a partial sit-up to lick his nipple. My tongue was sticking out, about to make contact when the doorbell rang followed by a series of knocks. Well, pounds, to be accurate. The bell rang over and over like someone was holding the buzzer and incessantly pounding on the door at the same time.

Dingdong Dingdong Dingdong—Bang Bang Bang.

Dingdong Dingdong Dingdong—Bang Bang Bang.

Dingdong Dingdong Dingdong—Bang Bang Bang.

I dropped back and blew out a frustrated breath. "I suppose one of us should get the door since it doesn't sound like whoever's out there is going away anytime soon. When I find out who's cockblocking me, I swear I'll..."

Oni stopped me with a gentle smile and a finger to my lips. "Hold that thought before you make any threats you can't take back, caveman. I strongly suspect I know who's here to see us."

I paled as I realized who he was referring to when I saw the mix of dread and amusement playing over his face. He scrambled off me and giggled as he ran for the door while I gave my cock a squeeze and slowly followed, after a quick adjustment to make sure I wasn't on display. Yeah, our guests didn't need know whether my cock was cut or not, and I was hard enough that they'd easily be able to tell if I didn't try to hide it.

Oni pulled the front door open just in time for me to walk up and meet the eyes of a pissy-looking Jun and a highly amused Tau. Jun barely spared me a glance, his attention immediately going to his son.

"Well, you look good, Oni. I'll give you that much. What were you thinking, baby? Running off and not sharing such a big moment with me? Didn't you think that I'd want to be part of your mating?" Jun hugged Oni tightly before standing back with a firm grip on both of his arms as he slowly gave his son the once-over.

I was nervous as fuck, not even sure how to respond—or if I should—when Oni solved it by speaking himself. He shrugged his dad's hands off and crossed his arms over his chest as he canted onto one hip and stared his dad in the eye. "Shared it with you? Why, did you want to watch? Maybe offer a few helpful tips?"

My eyes bulged out as I waited for Jun to explode. Instead, he shocked the hell out of me when he started laughing and hugged his son again. After he'd hugged Oni a few more times, he swatted his son's bottom and turned to yank me into a hug too. After he let me go, Jun patted my cheek with a strangely affectionate smile before turning back to Oni.

I stood there in confusion until Tau came over and slung an arm around my shoulders with a quiet chuckle. "Welcome to the family, son. Trust me, you'll get used to these two and how they interact. So, tell me. You got any coffee? Your dads are tea freaks like everyone else on this blasted continent. Give me a good cup of java, I always say."

While I went into the kitchen to make a pot of coffee, my doorbell rang again and my brothers and dads walked in. While everybody was busy fussing over Oni, his sister and her wives also showed up to join the party. Sammy bustled into the kitchen, rubbing his hands together. "Let me see what I can whip up for you to serve, it looks like everyone is staying for dinner."

My jaw clenched as I moved aside to let my brother have his way with my kitchen. I was still horny and more than a little pissed about our plans being put off to begin christening every room of the house.

I didn't realize how obvious I was being until my dad pulled me aside with a laugh. "Simmer down, cub. We don't all need to smell you to know you're horny. You're newly mated, so of course you are. Deal with it, just like the rest of us did once upon a time with our own families."

My papa came strolling over with a braying laugh. "No kidding. Ask your dad about our claiming night and what his family put us through."

Dad snorted. "Yeah, at least you don't have to wait for hours on end to watch me get crowned as a tribal alpha and sit through a ceremonial dinner before you can be alone with your mate. And you got to claim him and have a bit of a honeymoon before everybody descended on you, so you've already had it better than I did."

Papa grinned. "And bonus points if you made it through your claiming night with nobody getting a black eye or a bloodied nose."

Jun started laughing from across the room. "I've heard that story from Parker, but feel free to tell it again. I especially liked the part where you two virgins couldn't figure out what you were doing and ended up cracking an ancient Fae portal when you finally consummated things."

My brothers and I all groaned at the thought of our parents getting freaky. Lulu, on the other hand, had no problem with it. "Seriously? Your sex life had something to do with that whole portal thing? I'd never heard that part of it. I've only heard about the quests and how you all fixed it, not how it got messed up in the first place."

Papa shook his head. "It wasn't us fucking that did it." I fought the urge to plug my ears at the mention of fucking and my parents in the same breath while Papa blithely continued. "It was when we claimed each other. You see, the triplets were conceived in that moment. It was the mix of our double-dose of powers and the creation of whatever mix of power it is that these three contain that broke the agreement that had been signed in blood regarding the portal. Yep, that's what made it crack, and it was magical in origin. But then, aren't all those ancient things?"

"Speaking of getting a hole-in-one and conceiving on your claiming night," Lei interrupted. "Is anybody going to talk about the elephant in the room? Well, he's not really an elephant yet—we'll give him a couple months before he gets fat enough and that happens."

Oni silently flipped his sister the bird while everyone laughed. Jun was oblivious as he rushed over and began hugging Oni all over again. "How could I have gotten so excited that I forgot? We have so much to talk about, son. This baby will be here before we know it. There are a lot of preparations to be made." Jun's smile grew softer as he turned to hug my papa. "Oh, Clark. Can you believe we're going to be grandparents? And share a grandbaby?"

"I know," my dad crowed. "Isn't it exciting?"

Tau caught my eye with a shrug. "Like I said, welcome to the family. Get used to it, kid."

CHAPTER 8

ONI

Even through my pajama pants, the tile was cold against my ass as I hugged the toilet, my cheek resting on the rim of the seat. A strong kick had me glaring at my distended stomach, although I couldn't help the smile that escaped at the sight of what looked like a hand pushing against my taut, rubbery-looking skin that was stretched nearly to its breaking point over my baby mound.

Yeah, thank the goddess that I hadn't had a multiple pregnancy like Connor's family was known for... I couldn't imagine how much larger I would possibly be at this point if I were carrying twins or triplets. Or for that matter, how my body would even accommodate such a thing.

A giggle escaped me as I watched my belly button pop in and out like a turkey timer with each kick. Even though pregnancy made me grumpy, knowing my child was in there made up for it—almost.

"How are you doing, sweetness? You think you can get up yet?" Connor looked concerned as he walked in, his broad shoulders filling the doorway. "I'm so sorry this entire pregnancy has been so awful for you. I thought morning sickness was supposed to pass after the first part, you know?"

I groaned as I sat up and leaned back against the tub. "Ha! I wish it had only been morning sickness. Nobody told me it would be morning, noon, and night sickness. This is such bullshit."

Connor moved to the sink to dampen a pair of washcloths. I watched as he wrung them both out and neatly folded one of them into a rectangular strip before coming over and crouching beside me. "Lean forward, baby. You know this will help."

"Quit being so sweet. How can I call you my caveman when you have to go and be so damn precious with me?" I grumbled as I bent my head downward for him to lay the folded cloth over the back of my neck. With the other, he gently wiped my face and chest before tossing it into the hamper and pulling me into his arms.

"Have you seen the new trick your bellybutton is doing?" he asked after a few moments of silence. I looked down and snorted at the sight of my bellybutton doing the turkey timer bit again. "That is either the coolest or creepiest thing I've ever seen." Based on the sound of awe I heard in his voice, I figured he was probably thinking it was cool.

"I saw his hand a few minutes ago too; you just missed it." I rubbed a hand over my belly, tracing circles over the places I felt our son kicking.

"Dammit, I have the worst timing. At least I got to see the foot last night though, right? That was pretty cool." He rested his hand over mine, threading our fingers together as we cradled our baby. When both of our hands bounced, we started cracking up. "He's got to be an alpha, with kicks like that."

My head snapped to the side so fast that the washcloth went flying, landing with a splat on the tile beside me. "And now we're back to caveman. Have you forgotten how strong your omega brothers and friends are? Don't make me have to *omega out* on your ass."

Connor snorted. "Omega out? What, is that like Hulk out or something? Are you going to Hulk smash—or should I say *omega smash* my ass?" He paused and tapped a finger to his lips. "Although, now that I think about it... I'd like to hear more about what your plans are with my ass. That's intriguing, lamb chop."

Anything I would've said was halted by a loud gurgling in my stomach. Connor jumped to his feet and reached a hand down to help me up. "That's our cue. Time to feed the baby and his papa."

I whimpered as he helped me stand. "Yeah, by all means let's prime the pump so I can blow more chunks later."

Connor pulled me close for a soothing hug. "Don't worry, I

have all the ingredients laid out by the blender for your mint and pineapple smoothie. And if that one doesn't sound good, I can do a lemon ginger one instead, or even apple."

I rested my chin on his chest as I pouted up at him with a scrunched-up nose. "Can I vote neither? I don't care what my dad says, that shit is nasty. I mean, maybe if you swapped out the spinach you insist on adding in there for ice cream or something, it might be better."

Connor chuckled as he turned me around and marched me toward the door. "You need the iron and folate from the greens. Sorry, not sorry. I'll be happy to get you a scoop of ice cream later, if you think you can hold it down. Sammy brought over some sorbet he made with the same lemon ginger or mint and pineapple flavors that you prefer for your smoothies. I think he made a peppermint ice cream, too. I'll have to check the freezer, he stuck a bunch of tubs in there and told me they were for you. I kind of lost interest when he started listing ingredients though."

"For the record, I don't prefer any of those flavors for my smoothies. We both know that I prefer my smoothies to taste like candy bars, but at least these recipes my dad gave you seem to help the nausea a little."

As he guided me into the kitchen and led me to a stool at the counter, Connor brushed a kiss over my temple before scooting around to the blender. "I promise that once you're not puking all the time, I will happily make you all the chocolate peanut butter smoothies your heart desires."

"I mean, I think those are technically milkshakes, but I'll take it... after a month or so. Maybe a year. I don't know, but it's going to take me a long time to be able to look at a smoothie again after I pop this baby out." I shook my head at the thought as I absently rubbed a hand over my belly.

After he'd made my liquid breakfast, Connor set about straightening the kitchen while I sipped at it. I looked up at Connor after I looked at the ingredients in my glass. "You know, Baba laughed when he said that these things were the only thing that helped him through his miserable pregnancy with me. I can't help but wonder if a small part of him isn't finding poetic justice in watching me go through the same thing. Although, maybe it's a good sign? He wasn't sick at all during his pregnancy with my sister, and look at what a brat she turned out to be. Maybe our son will be sweet like me, you think?"

Connor threw his head back with a loud laugh. He was still shaking his head when he glanced over to see me frowning. He held up his hands. "Trust me, I'm not stupid enough to touch that one. But yes, you're definitely the sweet one... mostly."

I lifted a brow. "A wise man would've stopped before that last word, just saying."

He leaned over the counter to steal a kiss. "And I'm just saying that maybe I like a little salt with my sugar, Mr. Feisty."

When he reached for an apple and bit into it, I rolled my

eyes as I remembered our mission and took a drink. "Do you think we're ever going to find Atalanta's apple? I mean, we've been looking through every possible bit of lore handed down through the generations and there's nothing. Not even a thread. Your grandpa Frankie and my sister have both been scouring the internet. If those two techno-freaks can't find it, maybe it really doesn't exist."

Connor shook his head. "It has to exist, or the goddess wouldn't have put us on its trail. I mean, we could be following the wrong myth, but I don't think so. We all feel strongly that this is the one, so it definitely exists. We just have to find it and guard it. Easy peasy, remember?"

"I know, I'm just frustrated because it feels like we're just sitting here twiddling our thumbs while I grow larger by the second. The baby's due in three weeks; if we don't find a lead soon, I'll be out of commission when it comes to retrieving it."

"If it takes that long, we'll just wait until you're on your feet again. Because there's no doubt that we'll both need to be there. Easton wouldn't have included you if you weren't meant to be part of it. You said it yourself, our parents' quests were done in pairs, and it looks like history is repeating itself."

I sucked in a breath. "Parents! Shit. What time is everybody showing up? I wasted the whole morning hugging the porcelain god and we're hosting that barbecue to welcome our packmates who are visiting from England."

"Don't worry, precious. All you have to do is sit there and let everybody fuss over you. Your dad has insisted on doing the grilling and my family are bringing all the sides. Sammy has our refrigerator filled with pans of marinating meat. I'd show you, but you and I both know what happened the last time you smelled raw meat." Connor shuddered at the memory of that one. Not only had I not made it as far as the bathroom, but his shoes had been baptized—to put it kindly.

"Are you sure people won't think I'm playing the pregnancy card?" I chewed my lip, frustrated that I was so far from my normal self these days. I'd never been a guy to sit idly by while everyone else did the work, it just wasn't my style.

Connor smiled gently. "There is not a person around who'd ever think that of you. Shit, don't forget that Uncle Ansh is a diva's diva. If anything, he'll be upset that I'm not sitting at your side waving palm fronds or some shit like that."

I giggled at that idea. "Good point. Although now that you mention it," I frowned as though deep in thought, "palm fronds probably would give me a nice breeze. And I do get so hot."

"Nice try, but we both know you'd break my wrist if I tried something like that. Goddess, can you imagine the comments from your sister?"

"Now see, that just makes it more appealing," I laughed.

* * *

It was so good to see our friends again. Kyle and Jude didn't make it over here often enough for my liking. Kyle was hilarious, loud, and completely adorable. His twin, Jude, was his polar opposite. He was one of the most mellow, laid-back, and patient people I'd ever known. They were two of my favorite alphas on the planet, but then again, I felt that way about all my friends and pack "uncles." I just hadn't seen these ones as much lately. But sitting here with Connor and my pack around me, everything finally felt right with my world.

"Oni! How are you feeling? I've heard about your awful indigestion issues. I brought you an entire case of Chimes ginger chews. Not only are they a tasty candy, you'll find they work great for nausea. They really are quite a treat; I stumbled over them while we were traveling through Indonesia a few years back." My uncle River settled down in the chair beside me, passing me a package of candy as he spoke. "The rest of the case is in your kitchen, Connor assured me he would put it in a cool, dry place to store it."

His mate, my uncle Mark, shared an affectionate smile with River as he joined us. "I'll have you know that your uncle was determined that you were to have that candy. Believe it or not," he made a playful gasp, "he even sprang for express shipping so we'd have it in time for the trip."

We all laughed at that one. Uncle River was known for his distaste of capitalism in every form, but especially when companies extorted you for what he considered to be exorbitant shipping rates. I made a show of opening the package and unwrapping a candy. It didn't smell too awful, so I popped it in my mouth and patted my uncle's hand. "Thank you for your sacrifice, Uncle River."

He threw his long hair over his shoulder with a grin. "It wasn't a problem. I just closed my eyes when I hit enter. See no evil, hear no evil, right?"

"Yeah, because that works, Uncle River." Kyle dropped down on the ground beside my chair and snuck a candy out of my bag. His face screwed up as he spat the candy right back into his hand and tucked it back into its wrapper. "No offense, but yet again, I'm glad I'm not an omega if you guys have to deal with shit like that."

I shrugged. "If it settles my stomach, I'm all for it. Anything is better than puking my guts out day and night. Besides," I flashed a smile at my uncle, "it's not bad. Trust me, I've grown accustomed to the spicy taste of ginger. It pairs well with apple or lemon."

"Ooh! Speaking of apples, what's this I hear about you and Connor being on some big quest from the goddess? Are you guys trying to undo everything our parents did, or is this a do-over to show you can do it better?" Kyle reached out with a grin to take a beer from Jude's outstretched hand before looking back to hear my answer.

Jude gracefully lowered himself to the ground beside his

brother. "Are you allowed to talk about it? Don't let Kyle bully you into spilling the beans if it's not okay."

The rest of my adopted uncles and pack perked up at the topic and slowly meandered closer to hear what I had to say. Connor and his brothers all came and sat down on the grass near me while our parents took seats in the assorted lawn chairs. Connor rested a hand on my knee. "Tell them whatever you want, sweetie pie. I don't feel like we aren't allowed to discuss it freely. And it's not like we haven't already shared the details within our immediate families."

As I launched into our tale, all of my parents' generation smiled when Easton's name came up in conversation. Connor's uncle Parker shook his head. "That guy again? It figures he'd be hip deep in this one. Is he still banging the goddess? Or is it not okay to say that?"

Connor's papa started laughing at his brother's questions. "I'm pretty sure that nothing good can come of joking about the goddess' sex life."

My baba rolled his eyes as he settled onto my dad's lap. "Can we get back to the conversation at hand, please? The last thing I want to think about is anyone else's sex life, let alone that of a goddess and her Fae bae."

"Bae?" My sister snorted soda through her nose. "Please tell me that our honorable baba did not just say Fae bae." She shook her head. "Although, it does sound awesome, right? Say it three times fast in a high voice and you'd almost think you're hearing an ambulance siren."

"Anyway..." I said pointedly in an attempt to bring the conversation back around. "We followed the clue he gave us and it led us to the legend of Atalanta and her golden apple. The only problem is while her story has survived the ages, we can't find any record of an actual gold apple ever existing. And that's where we've been stuck for the past three months."

Kyle held up a hand, his eyes bulging with excitement. "When you say golden apple, are you meaning that it's a solid gold object or a basic, ordinary yellow delicious fruit? Because if you're talking about solid gold, I've freaking seen one matching that description in this series of recurring dreams I've been having. In fact, I just had the damn dream again last night."

Everyone grew silent as we turned to look at Kyle. Jude looked thoughtful for a moment. "Why don't you tell us about your dream? Because I'm pretty sure that nobody would dispute that there are no coincidences in this life."

Kyle rolled his eyes. "Jude, you're such a fucking hippie. But, you're not wrong. So this dream, it's crazy! It's like I'm looking at this dude who looks just like Father. He's dressed in like this kilt or loincloth-looking thing, but it's white linen. Oh, and he's got all these gold bracelets, a fancy necklace, and even gold sandals on his feet. He could totally be my father if he was trying to look like an ancient Egyptian, even down to having kohl lined around his eyes. But anyway, this Father-clone is standing in this room hiding it, looking around to make sure nobody is watching. I got the vibe that he'd stolen it or something, just by how secretive he was being."

My baba nodded gravely. "It sounds as though you have your father's gift for dreams. In our day, our group would form a circle, using our gifts to channel all of our powers so that your Uncle Kent could cast a dreamscape so we could all view the vision or dream that had been seen. You know, Kyle, it was your dad, Cody, who would hypnotize us into a dream state for this to happen." Baba paused to look at me and Connor. "Perhaps you kids might consider doing the same."

Kyle shook his head. "But I'm a precognitive dreamer. I've always had visions of the future in my dreams, not ancient shit."

Jude looked amused. "Have you never heard of ancestral memories? They often come in the form of dreams." He turned to look at his own father, my uncle Kontar. "Doesn't our family line come from Egypt, on your side?"

His father shrugged. "Yes, but I don't know much of my family history. I've heard a few things, but I was orphaned too young for my parents to instruct me. And as the last of my line, all I had to go on was hearsay from other shifters who'd known them. There are even rumors that we still own property somewhere over there that has been passed down through the generations, but if it exists, I've never seen a deed or laid eyes on it. I don't know that we really want to root into my family history though; what little I do know tells me that my ancestors were a bit unsavory in former generations."

"Unsavory? What the fuck does that mean, Father?" Kyle looked intrigued now.

Uncle Kontar chuckled softly. "Don't look so excited, son. When I say unsavory, I mean evil. My ancestors had great wealth, but they earned it through slavery. They sold their own brethren for their personal gain. Thieves, liars, and slavers—that's what my line is made of, or so I've been told."

Jude looked saddened by that as he frowned down at his lap. "I'm glad that recent generations have cleaned up their act, but it breaks my heart to know that we have that in our family history."

"Forget about all that, we can't undo the past. All we can do is do better in our future, everybody knows that. But you know what I do know?" Kyle pumped a victory fist high over his head. "I know that I smell an African excursion in our future, guys!"

I grinned at Kyle. The guy really did crack me up. "That's all well and good, but first we'll have to figure out where. Egypt is a broad area; we'll need to pinpoint a better location."

* * *

Connor spooned me from behind, his hand resting possessively over my belly as he slowly thrust into my welcoming heat. "How are you feeling now? You've had a long day, my love."

I smiled at that. Of all the myriad of endearments he used on me, "my love" was probably my favorite. I looked back over my shoulder. "Are we talking or fucking right now?"

With another gentle thrust, Connor nipped at my neck before flashing me a grin. "We can't do both?"

I bit back a moan as the fat head of his cock slid over that magical bundle of nerves inside my ass. "We can, but don't expect me to concentrate on stringing two coherent words together for very long."

"What about if I do this?" Connor grinned almost wickedly before bending to scrape his teeth along my omega gland. "Or little bit of this?" His hand wrapped around my dick and began to stroke in rhythm with the undulation of his hips.

His hand moved down to fondle my balls before sliding back up the length of my dick in a gentle caress. I gasped when his fist closed around it again, and I squirmed back against him, coaxing him to plunge in deeper and harder.

The fragrant scent of my slick meshed with the musky aroma of our sweat filled the air. My breath hitched as he grazed his teeth over my gland again before sucking a kiss on my neck. I could feel my body vibrating as my inner cat began to purr.

"Yessss... do more of that." I shivered as he blew a hot breath over my ear. I could already feel his knotting vortex beginning to swell with each stroke, sending frissons of scorching electricity through my body. I hissed through my teeth as my balls drew tight.

I began to writhe against my mate when another graze of his teeth pushed me over the edge. I was powerless to hold it back another second. My dick pulsed as I shot ribbons of cum onto the bed beside me.

"Fuckkkk, you and that vibrobutt are gonna be the death of me," Connor groaned as his knotting vortex fully inflated, locking us together as his cock began to pump liquid heat into my channel.

I gave a languorous sigh as I leaned back into his strong chest. This was my favorite place in the world—being wrapped in his arms and firmly stuck together. Connor's hands rested possessively over my belly as he pressed a soft kiss to my neck.

"Sleep well, my love. We have another big day ahead of us tomorrow when our friends come over." His voice was like velvet in my ear as I floated toward sleep's siren call.

"I will, dearest. I always do when I'm glued to my caveman," I whispered as I gave into the soft embrace of peaceful slumber.

CHAPTER 9

CONNOR

My jaguar chuffed happily as Oni and I lay together in the grass. The afternoon sun warmed our fur while the fresh, fragrant grass was pleasing to the nose. There was just something about the crisp autumn breeze mixed with the warm sunshine that had called our names. When Oni had suggested we shift and enjoy some alone time before our friends descended, I hadn't hesitated to jump on board with the idea.

I rested my chin over my thick, meaty paws and watched as my mate rolled onto his back to scratch an itch. His strong, compact body was covered in a beautiful golden coat, but it was his shaggy, reddish-brown and black mane that made me want to shift back to human form so I could run my fingers through it. As a human, Oni had jet-black hair with just a hint of red here and there in the right lighting. But in this form, the reds and browns meshed with the black into breathtaking beauty.

His eyes glowed bronze, a sign of the powers he'd inherited through his baba's legacy omega line. Whereas normal shifters had a standard yellow-gold glow to their eyes, we legacy descendants had colors distinctly our own. If I were to look into a mirror right now, I'd see my eyes were glowing purple with a golden ring around the pupil. The only reason I had two colors was because of my parents' dual powers that went back to their unique birth stories.

I pushed my thoughts aside when I scented visitors arriving. A large red-tailed hawk flew overhead, screeching as it circled a few loops above us before dive-bombing toward the ground, only to pull up at the last moment and gracefully settle onto the grass as a large dingo with royal-blue eyes and an adorable red panda, with what could only be described as an amber glow to her eyes, ran into the yard. Oni flopped back over onto his side, huffing out a low roar of greeting to his sister and her mates.

The red panda chittered as she ran forward to bump her head against Oni's. Lei would punch me if I dared say it aloud, but she really was the cutest creature. Other animals soon began filling the yard. The familiar tawny coats with black rosettes scattered over them that so closely matched my own caught my eye as my brothers arrived.

I rose to my feet when Kyle's leopard sprang forward, his silver eyes catching mine as he came over to rub up against me to say hello. A pair of wolves were next, followed by a coyote with Jude's distinctive turquoise eyes shining intelligently from its face.

Our friends rubbed up against each other, brushing their scents on one another before joyfully running around the yard and letting their animals play.

My cousin Toby's bear lumbered over, his purple eye glow setting him apart from the golden eyes of his sisters. My twin cousins, Faith and Destiny, were special in that Faith took after the jaguar genes in our family while Destiny was a brown bear like Toby and our omega fathers.

Phoenix and Aaron, though brothers, had different eye glows due to the fact that Phoenix was an alpha and had his dad's orange glow while omega Aaron had his papa's golden eyes since the legacy gift in Uncle River's line had died out in his father's generation. In order for the gifts to pass on, it went from alpha to alpha or omega to omega, but Uncle River's dad had been born alpha, ending his family's trait.

The last to arrive was Ian. That little Irish fox was always late, probably because he'd been lost in time with his nose in a book before shifting, truth be told. Lei tackled Ian as soon as he approached. The huffing noise I made was my cat's version of laughter as I watched the two of them tumble around the grass like a pair of cubs.

As the smallest of our group, they could only safely play

with each other. Just like our parents before us, we were an eclectic variety of shifters that somehow worked. We were friends, we were family—we were pack.

When Toby and Destiny stood on their hind legs and began wrestling a little too forcefully, Oni lurched to his feet with a loud roar. At once, both bears dropped back to all fours, dropping their heads meekly to stare at the ground. I relaxed into my shift and watched as my claws retracted and my furry paws became human hands once again.

Pushing up from the ground, I stood and brushed my hands off. "Okay, gang. I think that was Oni's cue that playtime is over. I have a basket full of old clothes you've all left here in the past. It's sitting over on the porch. Go ahead and change after you shift so we can get cracking."

After everybody had done as I requested, we made our way inside. Oni caught my eye as he walked up to me. "Should we do this at the table? If we put the leaves in, there should be enough seating, right?"

Lei rolled her eyes. "I don't think the length of the table has anything to do with where we park our butts, but point us toward the leaves and we can make it happen, preggo."

Oni stuck his tongue out at her. "The table has benches and plenty of seats for our butts to park, as you so sweetly put it. I was actually thinking of having enough room for us to not be wedged all up against each other. I'm assuming we'll be holding hands séance style, and I don't know about you, but I want elbow room."

My brothers were already pulling out the leaves to extend the table while I got drinks for everyone. Oni and Lei were playfully bickering over something or other when I joined them. Toby reached for the tray of drinks, tripping over his own feet at the last minute and falling against me. His stumble nearly made it all crash to the floor, but my brothers and I were quicker than mere gravity. Our eyes focused on the pitcher of iced tea and glasses of ice as we levitated them back onto the tray that was now hovering in midair.

Ian shook his head. "'Sure, and don't I love ta see these ones and their parlor tricks, eh?" For a nerdy bookworm, he had an Irishman's humor along with a streak of snark in him about a mile wide.

Jon flipped his middle finger to Ian while we maneuvered the tray through the air, letting it hover before slowly allowing it settle onto the table. "You want to see a parlor trick? I'll give you a parlor trick," Jon grinned. Sammy and I rolled our eyes as we took our seats and watched as Jon made the glasses rise again and go flying through the air before landing gently in front of each person at the table. When he made the pitcher rise as well and go around the circle to self-pour tea over the crackling ice in each glass, Ian began to slowly clap.

"Well done, boyo. Sure and if ya didn't show me." He caught my eye with a wink. I bit back a laugh as I realized that this had been his intention all along. Our friends had always loved to watch my brothers and I do the *Fantasia* routine with household objects.

Oni hadn't been amused when he'd walked in to see the kitchen floor being cleaned by a self-propelled broom and dustpan after we'd first moved in together, until he'd realized that I could follow it with a mop and neither of us would ever have to scrub the floor. He'd laughingly called it cheating, but had decided to allow it. Because let's face it, housework sucks.

Fingers snapped in front of my face. "Wake up, loser. No daydreaming, save that for your own time. You and your brothers are supposed to take us on a dreamscape, remember?" Lulu playfully rubbed her knuckles over my scalp in a rough noogie before scooting around the table to join her mates.

Oni nodded. "While I take exception with you calling my mate a loser, no matter how jokingly it was intended, I do agree that we need to get to the matter at hand." He held a hand to his mouth as his jaw cracked wide with a yawn. "Sorry. But yeah, I get sleepy in the afternoons so we should probably get to this, I think."

I turned to Jude. "Do you share your dad's skills in hypnosis? I was assuming so, but I probably should've asked you about it when we planned this last night. If you can pull us into a dream state while Kyle focuses on his vision, my brothers and I can pull us all in with him."

"Yes, I can do that, I should think. Oni was right, I think joining hands would be best so that our powers can flow through the circle." Jude looked around thoughtfully for a moment. "I don't think it matters too much where everybody sits since our powers will flow through the circuit. However, I do think that maybe one of the trips should sit beside Kyle. Since Destiny is gifted with remote viewing, she should sit on the other side. Perhaps if she's there, we will be able to see more of the area around the site of Kyle's dream and, more importantly, pinpoint where it is to return there."

"That works for me," Destiny easily agreed as she hopped up to go sit beside Kyle while my brother Sam quickly took the seat on the other side of him. Jon and I smothered smiles at Sammy's immediate acquiescence. Usually he tended to second-guess himself, but Kyle had a way of making everyone feel comfortable at his side.

"Should we light a candle or something?" Kyle bit his lip as he looked around the table. "I think we need a focal point, don't we?"

Jude shook his head as he took a seat directly across from Kyle and held his hands out to Jon and Aurora who sat on either side of him. "No. Just close your eyes and let your minds clear. Remember, once we are there, we have to follow the rules that the trips explained last night when we planned this experiment. No touching each other if we find ourselves in a dreamscape."

At our nods of agreement, he closed his eyes and a feeling of serenity flowed through the air. "Now let us begin. I would like for everybody to focus on letting their minds drift into a white space. Just listen to the sound of my voice while Kyle focuses on his dream. Kyle, I want you to think of your dream, and only that. Think about what you saw, the colors, textures, and auras of the room. Picture it in your head as you clear your mind and let yourself be slowly drawn back there. The trips will allow us to join you when the time is right. Just listen to my voice and let yourselves drift. When I tell you to open your eyes, we should all be standing in Kyle's dream."

Jude's melodic voice was soothing despite the heady current of powers I felt swirling around the room. Jude and Oni had been right, we'd made an open circuit. If I were more intrusive, I could follow the flavor of each power back to its source and borrow from it, if I wanted. My friends would probably be unsurprised to know that my brothers and I could do that, but we'd always refrained from going there. Too much power could never be a good thing. I shook my head, forcing the thoughts from my mind and focusing on Jude's voice again.

"...open your eyes and see where we are." My eyes popped open as Jude said that and sure enough, we were standing inside of an ancient home. The room was luxuriously appointed with heavy curtains and plump, colorful pillows. A guy who looked disturbingly similar to Kontar was lounged on a brocade bench wearing nothing more than jewels and a white, linen skirt while eating figs. His hairless chest was bare, but shone as if it had been rubbed with oil. A girl close to him in age sat beside him while she slowly rubbed a perfumed oil into her hair.

After a lifetime of dream walking, even I was impressed by the detail—right down to the heady perfume of her oil. I'd never entered a dream from the past, at least not one cast by someone else. I'd had my share of dreams from my own past that my brothers and I still visited from time to time, but we'd never gone back millennia. And especially not into an ancestral dream. Hell, I wasn't sure I even remembered they were a thing. I zeroed in when I realized the dude in the skirt was talking.

"I mean it, Neema. I'm sick to death of our parents kowtowing to that silly general who has taken our town hostage. Rhakotis is a peaceful fishing town, and he wants to make it into a bustling metropolis? Who in their right mind would want that?"

"Hush, Kesi. Your only problem with the creation of Alexandria is your fear that our family might lose its reign of wealth. More people means more ships. More ships means more money for the family coffers. Just think of all the product we can ship to far-off lands." My stomach curled at her words after having heard Uncle Kontar mention his family's history as slavers. Surely she wasn't referring to people as product?

"Alexandria, indeed. What kind of a narcissistic clown

names a city after himself? Mark my words, Neema. General Alexander will be lost to history. Nobody will remember his name, let alone his puffed-up attempt at making Rhakotis into a city. It will fall to shambles within a decade, and our family will once again rule the area. If only our parents would see it my way, and quit kissing his fuzzy Greek ass."

Neema laughed as she set the bottle of oil aside and reclined against her brother's chest. "You must keep such thoughts to yourself, Kesi. Whether or not your words prove to be true, right now the Greek has taken over and our parents are simply protecting the family by getting into his good graces. After the meal we shared last night, he allowed our family to keep our estate. Our wealth will remain intact, which is what our parents had in mind when they accepted his invitation. You need to learn to get your nose a little brown if you want to succeed and continue to prosper in this new political environment. I know you hate change—who doesn't? But we must at least pretend to accept his plans in order for our family to continue to thrive."

Her brother ran an agitated hand through his hair before flopping back against the pillows with a disgusted snort. "The man is a pig. I cannot believe they made us have dinner at his home. The Grecian scum are beneath us in every way. While they call themselves enlightened, I've yet to see them build lasting monuments like our pyramids. Our society is the one that is correct. His kind are just a bunch of blowhards who think they are above us as they sit around discussing their precious philosophies. At least tell me you gifted yourself a souvenir or two while we were there? Everything he owned was made of silver or gold. To my way of thinking, a trinket or two that wouldn't be missed was little payment for the suffering we endured by sitting at his table."

Neema tittered. "I would never do anything so foolish as to steal from the Greek general. Alexander is a great man, just ask him, he'll tell you." She rolled her eyes then stood and arched her back like a cat. "No, brother, I took no trinkets. I have my eyes on a larger prize than mere pretties. I plan to have our parents arrange a marriage for me with one of his ranking officers."

Kesi sat up with an expression of horror on his face. "Neema, no! Surely you wouldn't be so foolish as to soil our family line with Grecian genes. Besides, why would you want a husband who would be off fighting whatever war the Greeks decide to wage next?"

She gave her brother a slow wink. "That, my dear Kesi, is exactly why I would marry one of his officers. They have their own wealth, yet short lifespans. If our town does become the proud city of Alexandria that the general has proclaimed it shall, then I will be sitting pretty at the top of the heap. And even better? I'll be a wealthy, young widow who can do as I please after my husband stupidly gets himself killed fighting someone else's war. I keep telling you, brother dearest, you must think ahead and see the larger picture." She wagged her finger at Kesi. "And I'd better not hear of anything having been taken from the general's home last night, or you'll have me to deal with. I'll not have my plans disrupted by our family name being stained from your sins."

"Bah. Leave my quarters, I've heard enough of your nonsense for one evening." Kesi waved a dismissive hand at his sister before reaching for another fig.

"I mean it, Kesi. Do not dare ruin my plans or you will face my leopard. Her claws and teeth are much sharper than yours." She left the room in a huff while her brother stared after her with a look of distaste.

He shook his head and muttered under his breath. "My cat's claws and teeth would be sharper too if I honed them on whetstones and flint. Silly wench thinks I don't know her secrets? Bah. I have my own secrets though, don't I?"

We watched as he bent to stretch his arm under the chaise, reaching far back into the shadows and rooting around before pulling out a gold apple. Oni sucked in a breath, his hands coming to his mouth as he watched the ancient man polish the apple on his skirt and toss it negligently into the air like one would with an ordinary piece of fruit. He caught it with a laugh and tucked it close to his side. He picked up what looked like a flint knife, then walked over to the window and opened the curtains to show a night-time sky.

When he climbed through the window, we casually

walked through the brick walls that really didn't exist for us to see him walk about two meters away to the corner of the house. After furtively looking around as if to make sure he wasn't being watched, he used the knife to dig a hole under the edge of the foundation. He held the apple up to admire it a final time, then kissed its surface before dropping it in the hole and covering it over with dirt and tamping the ground flat to cover what he'd done.

When he crept back to the window and stopped to wash his hands in a standing bowl of water, Oni reached out to touch my arm. We all gasped as one as we found ourselves back at the table looking around at each other in disbelief. Oni shrugged. "Sorry if you guys weren't done yet, but I couldn't handle another minute of watching that asshole."

Even Jude smiled at that one. He shook his head sadly. "It pains me to think that our father descended from those people."

Kyle grinned across the table at his twin. "Chill out, dude. We've improved over the generations, or so I'd like to think."

As everyone started to talk over each other, I noticed Aaron had grabbed a pen from the sideboard behind him and was scribbling something on a napkin. "What are you doing there, pipsqueak?"

Aaron smiled at my use of his old nickname. As one of the younger members of our group, he'd always trailed behind us and tried to keep up. Although we were all adults now, childhood memories couldn't be forgotten.

He tapped his finger on the napkin. "While you guys were watching that bugger dig his hole, I was looking around at the night sky and surrounding area. I'm pretty sure that I can make us a map that will take us where we need to go. The only problem is, I'll probably need to be along for the ride. I'm not trying to insinuate myself into your adventure, it's just that my mapping skills are weaker at a distance. Let me get close, and I can get you within an inch of where you want to be."

Toby flashed a goofy grin at Aaron. "I know the gifts from your dad's omega line were lost with his dad, but I really think that your natural empathy and mapping skills show that you have at least a touch of whatever skills used to run in your line."

Aaron shrugged. "Either that or I have spent way too many nights during my family's travels staring at the skies and learning the star patterns around the world. But thank you for believing in me." Toby flushed bright red; my awkward cousin never took compliments well.

Ian distracted my thoughts when he began drumming his hands on the table. "If Aaron goes, we all go, right? Sure and you can't have an adventure without takin' all yer mates along for the ride, yeah?"

Lulu's eyes danced at the idea. "Yes! I totally vote we crash their adventure. Getting to quest like our parents did would rock."

Jude shook his head sadly. "It's too bad we don't have magical creatures like they did to visit first. Although, we could stop to visit Effie and Maon on the way just to make our own quest parallel with our parents'."

"Shut up," Kyle laughed. "You just like visiting their cottage. I have to admit though, I am a little jelly that we didn't get to see Effie's phoenix form before the goddess made her human. Although Maon does make some killer cookies, so that's always a draw for me."

I shook my head with a grin. "Visit them on your time, we need to find this damn apple."

Oni and I were drinking our breakfast smoothies when the girls came pounding at the front door. I knew it was them because I could hear them talking excitedly on the other side of the door. "Sit tight, babycakes. I'll let them in."

"Please, did you think I didn't already know that?" Oni smirked.

I grinned and dropped a kiss on the top of his head before walking over to open the door. They came rushing in with Aaron at their heels. Lei brushed past me as she headed for the table and opened up her laptop the second her butt made contact with the chair. "Come on in, Lei. Make yourself at home," I quipped as I followed her to the table with everyone else at our heels.

"Shh, Connor. You just wait until you see what my girl found," Lulu said excitedly.

"With Aaron's help," Aurora pointed out.

Aaron shrugged. "I don't need recognition, it's enough that we were able to make this important discovery."

"What's going on?" I asked as I sat down beside Oni and looked around at their excited faces.

"What's going on is that not only do we have coordinates, I found Uncle Kontar's family land. It's not a myth, it really exists. I can't wait to tell him the news." Lei spoke in a rush as her fingers danced over the keyboard.

Lulu bobbed her head up and down, a stray feather catching my eye and making me smile. She'd been doing that since she was a baby, letting feathers from her bird form show in her human hair for decoration. "My girl had to search through a lot of databases to find it, but it's still registered to his family's name. We even saw it on Google Earth; that's what Lei's about to show you."

Lei blew her mate a kiss and nodded triumphantly as she turned the laptop around for us to see the screen. The land itself was barren without much more than what looked like a large pile of rubble at the center. As she zoomed in, we could see bits of stone and pillar from the partial building that remained. As we all stared in awe, Oni tugged at my shirtsleeve.

"Get your phone out, Connor. You need to get Kyle and Jude over here to see this and we need to start planning the trip. This baby is coming in three weeks. If we're going to go before he arrives, we need to get on it."

Our guests looked at us expectantly when Lulu spoke in an uncharacteristically quiet voice. "You guys *are* going to let us come along, right?"

"Bless you." Aurora smiled when I sneezed. The dry, dusty air was tickling my nose, despite how close we were to the Nile. She looped her arm through mine as we trekked onto Kyle and Jude's ancestral family lands. She lifted a brow when I started to giggle.

I shook my head. "Sorry, it just occurred to me that if any humans are watching or a satellite happens along overhead, it will look mighty odd to see a group of naked people walking through the dirt. We really didn't think this out too well, did we?"

"Hey, at least I brought a bag of sandals for us," Sammy commented with a glance at our feet. That only made me giggle harder. Something about a bunch of naked people wearing shoes was just a joke needing to happen. "Are you feeling okay? It's not the baby, is it?" Sammy asked softly when I winced and rubbed my belly.

"I'm fine, just laughed too hard, probably," I said quickly before Connor could pick up on our conversation. While our shifter ears could hear things a mile away, he was fortunately engaged in an animated conversation with Kyle and Jon. Truth be told, I'd been having twinges ever since we'd stepped off the plane, and they'd been growing worse as the day progressed. But I wasn't about to prove my baba right.

As if reading my mind, Aurora smiled gently. "I know your baba was concerned about you traveling so close to your due date, but you've still got nearly two and a half weeks left before he arrives, right?"

"Exactly, no worries here. If I were having multiples, I'd be concerned about them coming early, but I'm not, so everything is copacetic." I shuddered as we drew closer to the old pile of rubble. I couldn't put my finger on it, but the place had a feeling of malevolence to it.

Connor slowed and turned back to see where I was, then stopped to wait for me to catch up. "I'm sorry, sugarbear. I got caught up in conversation and ignored you; that was rude of me."

I took his hand with a smile and resisted the urge to roll my eyes. "We are mates, Connor, but we aren't joined at the hips. You're allowed to talk to our friends sometimes without me right there with you."

He lifted my hand to kiss my palm. "But there's nowhere else I'd want you to be, sweetness."

"Gag. Do you have any of those ginger candies on you?" Kyle joked. "Those things taste nasty as fuck but they'd be better than having to swallow hearing Connor gushing over you. Nope, guess not. Nowhere to hide them now, I suppose. At least, nowhere I'd want to put my mouth. Now Connor, on the other hand…"

I wiggled my pinky at Kyle, because his comment wasn't worth giving him the full bird—he only got the tail feather. He grinned at our old joke. "You missed it, I was just telling your man here about how amazed our dads were to hear about this place. They plan to make a trip here in the near future to see it in person. Father will have to decide what to do with the land, because leaving it sitting here fallow like this is just sad."

"Especially when you remember the dreamscape and how it looked in its heyday. It's crazy when you see it now," Jude commented as he looked around. "Take a deep breath, gang. You can literally smell the history."

I was growing more uncomfortable the closer we got to the pile of rubble. No offense to my friends, but this place had bad auras. There was a murky black cloud over the building. I realized that Lulu and the trips could see it too when I noticed them each looking askance at it, then glancing away. Lulu's zany streak was dialed way back; she seemed almost more timid with every step that took us closer to the dark rubble.

Jude surprised me when he spoke. "I think when our dads come to see this, they need to see what can be done to reclaim the property and put it to a better use. Maybe we can find a way to wash away some of the bad juju I'm picking up."

Even Kyle seemed subdued. "Yeah, why don't we grab that prize you're seeking and get the hell out of Dodge. That seems like the best plan to me."

Connor slid a stabilizing arm around my shoulder when I stumbled over a rock, anchoring me against his side to steady me. When we reached the corner of the building we were seeking, everyone stopped and formed a semi-circle around me and the trips. I had no idea why I needed to be involved, other than being Connor's mate. But he insistently took my hand as he and his brothers joined hands.

The trips stared at the dirt that hadn't been disturbed in centuries. Almost instantly, the dirt began lifting up and pouring aside as if being tumbled through by an invisible auger. I forgot all about the black cloud and bad juju as I watched the dull, dirty, golden apple emerge from the ground. It flew up from the hole in an arc. As it fell toward me, I instinctively stretched my hand out and neatly caught it.

I trembled from the powerful vibes coming from it—both pure and evil—and fumbled it. Before it hit the ground, my sister sprang forward and caught it. Her eyes rolled back as her retrocognitive powers read the object's history in a flash. I knew from hearing her speak in the past that she was seeing flashes of every person who'd held it. Her eyes fluttered back to normal and she gave a violent shiver before tossing it toward the trips.

Connor caught it first, his eyes closing as he used his own powers to absorb whatever information it was giving him. He tossed it in the air and levitated it toward Jon, who did the same object reading before passing it up and levitating it to Sammy.

While Sammy read it, I huffed with exasperation. "Seriously. Aren't you guys getting a little old for these parlor tricks? Is somebody going to tell us what you've seen? All I picked up was a mix of good and evil."

"It is Atalanta's golden apple—the warrior's prize," Lulu said quietly. "I'm not sure whether I'm happy or sad for her. She was thrilled when her love won the race and she knew that not only could they be together at last but she wouldn't have to kill him. However, she was equally heartbroken. The moment he won, the power in her body dissipated and she lost it all for love. And you don't want to know the half of where it went between her time and Alexander the Great. Let's just say that this thing has always been used by people with ulterior motives or stolen by people like Kesi."

"I don't care about all that, I suppose. But tell me one thing." I glanced at her curiously, ignoring my mate and his brothers who were playing some form of levitation-style catch with the apple. "How the heck did it get into the hands of Alexander the Great?"

Connor glanced over his shoulder with a grin before she could answer. "Believe it or not, he won it in a bet with Caesar himself."

"Enough playing around." Lulu shivered again as she hugged herself and rubbed her arms. "Can we maybe move things along?"

Connor and his brothers had left the apple floating in midair while they were distracted by the house. They'd righted some of the fallen pillars with their powers and put some of the stones back in place. They'd worked fast, the stones moving into place with just a thought from them, it seemed, and it was already beginning to resemble the house we'd seen in our dreamscape.

Sammy walked over and plucked the apple out of the air, tucking it into a woven bag he'd worn around his neck even when we'd shifted to make the excursion here in animal form since the place wasn't easily accessible. He'd no sooner put the apple away when all of a sudden, the ground began to shake.

"Earthquake! Everybody move your asses, we need to get away from the building!" Connor shouted as he ran over to lift me protectively into his arms while we all ran away from the precariously balanced pillars and stones. As we ran, the dirt was rolling like waves on the ocean and dirt geysers were blowing up from the ground and blocking our path as they blew straight up in the air in columns of dirt so high they could easily rival Old Faithful.

Connor stood me up and pushed me behind his back as everyone instinctively huddled together in a circle, standing shoulder to shoulder, facing outward with me kept protectively in the center. Connor and my sister stood directly in front of me, which didn't surprise me a bit.

I'd nearly forgotten my friend, Phoenix, was there until he yelled over the noise of the rumbling earth. "I thought Mr. Sandman was supposed to bring you a dream! These monstrosities are the stuff of nightmares!"

Some of the larger shifters in our group switched to animal form and began growling as an army of sandmen rose from the ground. From what I could see between Connor and Lei's shoulders, the fuckers had to be at least seven feet tall.

"What the actual fuck are those things," Lulu breathed in horrified fascination.

"Fuck me, but I think we're dealing with bloody golems," Ian answered. As the army of sandmen grew closer, the two bears in our group jumped protectively forward to start battling. I wanted to shift to my lion, but the cramps in my stomach were so bad now that I was afraid I'd hurt the baby if I shifted. I had no idea whether or not that was a good idea and I hadn't thought to ask my dad, the one person I knew who was an actual doctor.

While the larger shifters in our group fought the sandmen, more sprang forward before the ones they'd wounded fell to the ground. "Fall back," Jon shouted as the other trips lifted their hands to pull a wall of sand out of the ground. "Shit, I don't think it's gonna hold, guys." Jon's face was red from exertion as he held his palms out toward the wall.

Connor shook his head, grunting his words as if straining with all his might. "No, there are already cracks forming. Look at it, some of the suckers are breaking through already. We won't be able to hold it long, we need to figure something else out. You think we could levitate everybody out of here?"

"Fuck, no. I know I'm not the only one who saw that black-ass cloud overhead," Jon answered. "There's nothing good about that shit."

"What cloud?" Aaron asked nervously.

"Forget the cloud or whatever, I think I have an idea," Jude said as he pushed his way around to the trips. "You need to lower the wall. Do you trust me?"

Jon and Sam shared a smile while Connor rolled his eyes at them and answered Jude's question. "You know we do. Any one of us would trust you with our lives. I hope you have a better idea than we did, because I'm at a loss."

The wall dropped at once, sand fluttering to the ground like a magician's silken cloth. The huge golems began charging forward again until Jude held up a hand and confidently called out a single word. "Pavo."

The sandmen froze in place like statues. In the center of

the line, the largest golem's mouth fell open and a massive, earthen tongue rolled out. Sitting in the curl at its tip was a dull metal disc. We all cringed when Jude matter-of-factly stepped forward and retrieved it. As soon as he'd removed it, the entire army disintegrated into a giant cloud of dust. It was like a mini sandstorm blew over the place before it all slowly settled back to the ground. Before the air cleared, I happened to glance across the field to where a familiar woman stood on the southern end, watching with a frustrated scowl.

It took me a moment to place her before I realized that it was the waitress who'd been so rude to us that morning back in Greece. I started to say something to Connor, but Jude was trying to hand him the disc. "Check it out, it's some sort of ancient coin."

Connor shook his head and held up a hand. "Keep it for now, it might be a clue of some sort, but I feel like you were the one who was meant to find it since you were the one who was shown what to do."

I was about to mention the waitress, but I noticed she'd gone. Before I could say a word, I started to choke from the dust in the air and began coughing, just like everyone around me. I was mid-cough when a gush of water splashed my bare legs. "No! Not here! And definitely not now, I'm not ready, dammit!" I was freaking out, trying to quit choking while I stared pitifully at the ground. It was too late; my water had broken.

"It's okay, Oni-bologna," Phoenix said softly. "We can

deliver the baby right here; Aaron and I have had to help our dad deliver more than one baby during our travels over the years. You'll be fine, I promise."

I bent over double from a massive pain spasm, clutching my belly protectively as I shook my head from side to side. "No. I don't care what it takes, but my baby will not be born on land with bad juju."

"Easily solved, my darling." Connor scooped me up and jogged across the field toward where the Nile flowed on the west side of the property. Once we'd stepped off the land, I felt immediately better. Connor carried me over to the riverbank and lowered me to the ground as another pain racked my body.

Phoenix gently nudged Connor aside. "Don't kill me for getting all up in your man's business, but someone needs to deliver your son."

As I gave birth beside the ancient river, most of our group washed the dirt off their naked bodies in the river. Phoenix pulled my son free and passed him into my arms, while Aaron pulled the cord taut as Connor extended his finger and transformed it into a claw to cut it. Sammy conjured a bandanna from the bottom of his bag and got it wet to clean some of the muck from the baby.

I blew out a breath and shook my head at Connor. "I really hate it when my baba is right. This little shit couldn't have waited to go full term? You know we're never going to live this down, right? And now we're cleaning him with filthy river water?"

Connor chuckled as he rested a hand over the back of our son's head and kissed my cheek. "We have things on the plane to clean him properly, my love. This is just getting the worst of it off him. As for your dad being right? I can live with that, since our son is healthy. Just listen to those lungs."

I smiled at our screaming little alpha lion. It seemed as though he was declaring his rage at having left the nurturing warmth of my womb to anybody who would listen.

"I still can't believe you didn't have multiples," Jon said with a grin. "You rebels are like the black sheep of the family now, you know that, right?"

"Screw that, if they want multiples, then they can carry them. I'm good with one." I shivered at the idea of giving birth to multiples right about now. One had been bad enough.

Connor shrugged. "Hey, maybe the fates finally decided it was cool to let us chill with overpopulating the world from our family alone, you know?"

"What are you naming my nephew? I think that's the important topic to discuss." Lei dropped down on the ground beside me to admire my son. "I think you should go with Kojo because he was born on a Monday."

"Please don't," Lulu laughed. "It sounds too much like Kujo. I mean, can you imagine the jokes? Every time he shifted, the other kids would be checking him for rabies drool."

Connor laughed. "But just think about the rabies pranks he could pull; I could totally hook him up with some ideas there."

"How about a normal name?" I frowned. "I don't know, maybe something like Clyde or Horace."

Connor quirked an eyebrow. "What I'm hearing is that you want me to name him and any other children we have. Is that what you said? Because that's what I heard."

"You know, I know a cool Nigerian name that means born on the road or born during travel. What you think of Ode?" Jude smiled gently at the baby as he spoke.

"Definitely not." Lei shook her head. "I remember hearing that also means dumb in Nigeria, so we're not doing that to my nephew either." She paused for a moment, her eyes lighting up as a thought occurred to her. "Oni! What do you think of Dylan? That name comes from a sea god, so it literally means son of the sea. And since he was born on the bank of the Nile, it kinda fits. Plus, it's normal like you wanted."

"Yes! I like it. What do you think, Connor?" I searched his eyes for any sign of his agreement. Naming our son was pretty important, after all. We'd thought we had more time to figure one out before he arrived, but apparently the brat had other ideas.

"I love it." Connor bent to kiss our son's head. "Hello, Dylan. Welcome to our pack."

Oni looked less than thrilled as his proud baba toted our son around the party, showing his grandson off to all of our uncles and telling anyone who would listen that he'd told his son not to travel while pregnant. But did he listen? Hell, no. The poor child was born on the side of a damn river. The fact that his grandson was perfect was beside the point.

"Come here, silly boy." I pulled Oni onto my lap. "We already knew your baba was going to say I told you so, since he actually did."

"I don't know if I'm more bothered by that or the fact that he's the one showing off my baby. Doesn't Baba think that maybe I want to show Dylan to everybody? Or you," he added quickly. "I mean, he is *our* baby, after all. And what's with the shit of him being born by a river? Half our generation were born during their own quests. Hell, look where I was born!"

"Honeybunch, I will never pretend to understand your relationship with your baba, but I'm pretty sure that you're just as happy to see him so proud and thrilled with Dylan as you are irritated with his need to be right all the time." I nuzzled his neck, making him squirm with a giggle.

"Fine, you're not wrong, I suppose," he huffed. "But don't think I'm not taking Dylan on a second circuit to show him off the moment I get my hands on him again."

"Hey, Kent! It's your turn to tell us all how it feels for you and Clark to be the first grandparents in our group. We've already heard it from Tau and Jun, but Dylan's your grandkid too. Tell us how it feels, man." Uncle Cody grinned at my dad.

"It feels fanfuckingtastic," Dad replied with a smile that lit up the room. He turned to my papa. "We need to call our dads! I know they've already seen Dylan on video chat, but have we remembered to rub in the fact that they're great-grandparents now?"

Everyone in the room laughed because we all knew damn well that nobody would ever believe any of them were grandparents, let alone great-grandparents, due to our unique longevity. My papa grinned as he stepped up behind Dad and wrapped his arms around his mate's waist, resting his chin on Dad's shoulder. "Trust me, I've already pointed that out to Drew more than once."

Uncle Peter threw his head back with a laugh. "Why the

hell would you go and do that? My poor dad must have freaked."

Uncle Parker and my papa shared a smile before Papa smirked at Uncle Peter. "Someone had to pay him back for that misbegotten baby shower he threw you guys for the girls. Even though he apologized later, I had to get my twins back."

"Yeah, over two decades later," Uncle Parker chuckled. "That water is so far under the bridge that it's not even a puddle, Clark."

Oni nestled closer to me as we watched and listened to all the conversations swirling around us as our pack reconnected to share our joy. It was nice of my dads to throw us this big party, but it was even nicer to be able to be here to celebrate.

As though reading my mind, Oni glanced up to meet my eyes. "I'm glad our adventure is over. The apple is securely tucked away in your safe with the biometric lock and enough wards to confuse even a coven of Fae warlocks, if such a thing exists. Our part is done, freaky golems and all. Now we can sit back and enjoy our son. I feel like we've barely had a moment to breathe since we've been together. It'll be nice to be just the three of us for a bit, don't you think?"

I started to say something about how now that it had begun, it wouldn't be long before the next quest was delivered when Jude stumbled past us, sniffing the air. He glanced over at us, his eyes frantic as he tried to figure out what he was scenting. "Do you guys smell that? What is it? Oh my goddess, it's like smelling the best solstice memories, and home, and love, and... fuck. I don't even know what it is except it's just about everything good in the world all wrapped into one big ball of deliciousness that smells vaguely of pine." He shook his head absently. "I'll talk to you guys later; I need to track the scent down and maybe let my coyote out to roll around in it for a while."

"What the hell is he going on about?" Oni asked as he watched Jude wander away with his nose in the air, continuing to sniff loudly as he roamed the room.

"Think about it, pumpkin. Remember the night you scented me? I'm pretty sure that my brother's mate just figured it out." I answered through our connection so as not to be overheard. Oni sat up straight and stared at me with wide, excited eyes.

"Jude is going to be our brother-in-law? That's fantastic news." Oni's eyes were bright as he watched. *"But which brother is his mate?"*

I tapped the tip of his nose with my fingertip. *"Despite my rules, I could probably tell you now, my love—but I won't. Trust me, you'll enjoy it so much more seeing it happen for yourself. Just watch and see because he's about to figure it out."*

Oni squealed and bounced on my lap as Jude flung himself at my brother, pulling his omega in for a big hug as he buried his face into my ecstatic brother's omega gland, oblivious to the fact that everyone in the room was watching and enjoying the show.

I pulled Oni back against my chest and nuzzled over his claiming mark. "I'm so glad I have you to share these moments with, my love. I hope you know that you're everything to me."

He turned to kiss my cheek. "As you are to me, Connor. You're my mate, my love, my everything. Or, as Jude so aptly put it, just about everything good in the world all wrapped into one big ball of deliciousness."

Artist Wanted... Canvas ready for your Shibari expertise

Join my mailing list and get your FREE copy of Artist Wanted
https://dl.bookfunnel.com/smahgmeo1v

Twitter:
https://twitter.com/SusiHawkeAuthor

Facebook:
https://www.facebook.com/SusiHawkeAuthor